A BIRD'S-EYE VIEW

A NEW STORY FROM THE MIND OF

ERIC RICKEY

Shirley Jean Publications

Layout and design by Jennifer Cartright
Cover design by Michael Cartright

This book was made in conjunction with Go!Press, a division of auxarczen. If you have a book you would like to publish, contact us at auxarczen.com

cover images courtesy of vecteezy.com

ISBN: 9798218745028

First Edition

Shirley Jean Publications

This book is dedicated to

Anyone with thoughts of suicide and victims of domestic violence. There are people that care about you and want to help.

I love you!

A BIRD'S-EYE VIEW

Sammy Walker

Beams of sunlight radiate through the gap between the curtains, causing me to cover my eyes as I slowly blink them awake. Instantly, I recognize the warmth of the room. While I'm still covered, I feel hot and notice the sweat on my neck. Fearing the result, I reach to the nightstand for my phone. It's a quarter after eight, and I must've forgotten to set my alarm. Now, I've overslept and missed her. I hoped to be out of bed to see my mom off to work this morning. She's been working two jobs and I, myself, have worked every night this week. Outside of texting, or the random phone call, we haven't truly connected in a while. It would've been nice to have spent some time with her this morning. I miss her and I know she's also lonely. I'm not the only one that was isolated in this town because of my decision. She stood by me and was outcast right along with me. She lost almost every single one of her friends and I hate it for her. People just aren't friendly with us anymore.

I toss the blankets from my body and stretch out in

bed. The feeling I receive from my bones popping is rewarding. I yawn loudly and shake my full body before rolling to my side for a comfortable cuddle with my doggy, Milo. In return, he stiffens his front paws and pushes the pillows overhead as he stretches his lower half as far as his legs will allow. His mouth opens wide as he yawns dramatically. I smell his breath. It's awful, almost rancid even, and has been a point of conversation with mom and me. Neither of us has figured out why it's been so bad lately, or what we can to do about it. We've brushed his teeth and given him treats that were supposed to help, but none of it worked. I need to get him to the vet to see what she thinks, but I just don't have the extra money. Things have been tight lately and I'm saving for college. While I wait for my junior year to begin, I save every dime I get, and I know I have little to spare. To be honest, his breath is so horrible that I think I'm going to need to take him, anyway. I cannot stand the idea that it gets in the way of our precious cuddle time.

I sit upright and put my feet on the floor. The glaring sunlight blazing through the window is blinding, and the heat inside the room is overwhelming. Our A/C unit freezes up throughout the night and my mother usually shuts it off in the morning to let it thaw. She says it's low on coolant and we haven't had the money to get someone to come by to look at it. I don't know what that means, but she's usually pretty good at turning it on before leaving for work. However, this is not the first time she's forgotten. It just sucks that it's supposed to be the hottest day on record, and I think it's already over ninety degrees outside, at eight in the morning.

Not able to bear the temperature or the blinding sunrays any longer, I rise from the bed and slide my house shoes over my feet before walking toward the door. Ready to join me and face our day, Milo leaps to the floor, catching me at the doorway. After exiting to the hallway, I turn left, toward the thermostat, and watch with joy as Milo spins in a circle before rushing back to my side. He pushes his snout firmly against my thigh. Perhaps to let me know that he's with me, but I don't know. He's a peculiar animal. Knowing our morning routine, he thought we were off to potty before meeting in the kitchen for our breakfast, but I fooled him. I chuckle to myself as I watch him wait patiently, with his nose pressed against my leg, and his eyes turned upward, curiously watching me.

Just as I suspected. The air is off and the temperature inside the house is almost eighty degrees. I slide the knob to cool and turn toward the kitchen. Milo, feeling that he knows our destination, bounds ahead while peering back to ensure I follow. Again, I fool him and duck in the bathroom. After pulling off a large wad of toilet paper, I blow my nose. I catch a glimpse of him as he sticks his face around the corner, watching me with confusion. It was miserable last night with this stuffy nose, and I'm barely able to breathe. Mom says I have a summer cold and I don't like it. I've never been sick in the middle of summer before and it actually feels worse than in the winter. I don't think a person is supposed to get a stuffy nose during the summer. It's just not fair.

After exiting the bathroom, I lead Milo to the back door and hold it open for him to exit into the yard. I follow behind and stand on the patio as he rushes into the yard to relieve himself. The sun, especially on this side of the house, is brutal this morning. It feels as if it's a million miles wide and shines brightly in the sky. While shading my eyes with my hand, I glance up and cannot find a single cloud in sight. I shuffle my feet. The pavers have warmed from the beating sun and I feel the heat radiating through the slim sole of my house shoe. Luckily, Milo is quick with his business and returns to my side, ready to return indoors.

We finally make our way to the kitchen and he sits

patiently, waiting for me to dish a helping of food in his bowl. As he eats, I pull a water bottle from the fridge and take a long drink. It tastes good, but it's freezing cold and I need to allow my mouth an opportunity to warm before taking another sip. After I've satisfied my thirst, I retrieve a bowl from the cabinet and a box of cornflakes from the cupboard. After filling it with milk, I fight the urge to add a spoonful of sugar. I really like it with sugar sprinkled across the top, but I've recently put myself on a diet. Over the past year, I've gained more weight, and I don't like how I look, or how I feel. Sugar is the first item on my list to reduce. It should be easy, but I'm a sucker for sweets. I like everything sweet. I like my tea sweet, my cereal sweet, and I even like sugar in my breakfast rice, with a little butter of course. The sweeter it is, the better it tastes. That's my opinion, anyway.

I win a minor victory and scurry off to the living room before I change my mind and add the sugar. After placing my bowl on the coffee table, I cross the room and retrieve the remote from the TV stand before returning to the sofa. As I power on the television, I scoop out a bite of corn flakes. I don't want to take too long since I don't like it when they get soggy. I'll still eat them, but they're not very enjoyable. With the television turned on, I log into the app, eager to get back to my show. I'm on my third pass through of Game of Thrones and I enjoy every minute of it. To be honest, I like the books better but the visual representation is really good too. If nothing else, I can get lost in the seven kingdoms for the next few hours and worry about nothing else. With my mother already off to work, I'm able to turn the volume to an obscene level and enjoy every moment of cinematic beauty as I drift away to another realm.

Just as I cross my legs and sit back with my bowl of cereal in my lap, Milo jumps to the sofa next to me. Unable to hide my joy, I smile and watch as he circles twice before plopping down and curling up. I feel immense love as stares at me with his big black eyes.

After I've spooned the last of the cornflakes from the bowl, I win another battle by placing it back on the coffee table, without drinking the milk. If I keep this up, I think, I might drop a few pounds before returning to school. It's just a few weeks away and I dread the idea. I wish my mother could stay home and give me the opportunity to homeschool, but that's not an option for us. I lay down on the sofa and pull the blanket from the back. Although it's still warm in the house, I like to cover up while I watch television and Milo loves to get under the blankets. He stirs as I stretch out and slide the blanket over the top of me. He stands to his feet and waits patiently for me to get comfortable. After making eye contact with him, he cautiously climbs up my legs and nestles between me and the back of the sofa. I lift the edge of the blanket as he wiggles higher, to where his head rests just below my armpit. I cover him up, and as I lay the blanket around his face, I giggle loudly as I draw a comparison, in my mind, between him and ET. Specifically, the spot in the movie where he's in the basket, on the bike, with the blanket around his face. He's such a cutie and I love him.

Milo, noticing my enjoyment, can't help but lick at my arm as he continues to gain comfort by wiggling around and getting lower into the sofa. The smell immediately hits my nose and I shy away. I feel terrible about it because I love him so much and he's my best friend. Honestly, he's my only friend. Sure, I have my mom and my grandma, but I don't think they count in that regard. He's my buddy and I talk to him more than everyone else, combined. Since I've gone through my transition, nobody seems to like me and he's all that I have. Milo is a pit bull mixed with something, and just like me, he's been abused. We got him from a shelter and he's been my best friend ever since. He's a smaller pit, skinny but muscular. He has a short snout and big black eyes to match his black fur. I don't know if it's a thing or not, but I'm pretty sure he's autistic. He just doesn't act like other dogs. He has no aggression, and he's very timid around people. My mom has been around him since we brought him home, and she's always treated him well, but Milo is timid around her as well. Maybe not as shy as he is with other people, but enough to wonder if he has anxiety issues.

I reach my hand down and rub his head while professing my love for him, and within moments, his eyes close. My heart is full, and he is content. The noise generated from the television is almost deafening as an incredible fight scene plays out. I glance down to catch a glimpse of my phone flashing from the coffee table. Not wanting to disturb Milo's rest, I carefully reach out to the table, while using my fingertips, and slide my phone closer. Once it's within reach, I pick it up and hold it to my eyesight.

It's a text from my mom, letting me know she left money on the counter for me to get medicine to treat my cold. I don't think I'll take it. I get paid today and will buy my own medicine. Mom can use her money for something else. Lord knows the electric bill is high with this run of continual high temperatures. Plus, she's always done everything for me and I want to help out around here, too.

I reach for the remote and pause the show while I text her back. I can't think with all the noise and I don't want to miss a minute. We're at a good part.

"Thank you. I'll stop by the pharmacy when I leave grandma's. Are you off work tomorrow? I miss you and would like to go do something together. Maybe go to lunch?"

I drop my phone to my stomach and resume play. I'm unable to contain my smile as a sword fight continues to play out in front of me. I really like this show. Almost immediately, my phone dings with my mom's response.

"I'm off all day. That would be nice. Miss you too. Let's get lunch and we can get some school shopping done. What are you doing today?"

"I'm going to grandma's for lunch and I have to pick up my new uniforms. I offered to help out today at the nursing home."

I don't want to go clothes shopping. I hate it. I always feel so uncomfortable and I hate my body.

"K. See you tonight. Love you."

I sigh aloud as I dread what I need to tell her next. She's going to worry and I don't want her to. She has enough on her plate and I don't want to add to it. I again pause the television.

"I won't be home till late. I'm meeting up with Ally and the guys and going to a party with them."

I hold my phone as I wait for her response, which again is almost immediate.

"When? Where? Are you sure that's a good idea?"

Just as I turn my phone to text back, it rings in my hand.

"Hello."

"Why didn't you tell me about that?" she asks, and I hear the concern in her voice. "I don't think it's a good idea."

I know she's worried about me and I'm nervous, too. "It'll be OK," I assure her. "What's the worst that can happen?"

She's quiet on the other end for a while. I hear a commotion in the background and know that she's needed to help. I hate when she feels the need to call me. She worries too much.

"How did this come about?" She asks. "I thought they didn't like you and were bullying you last year. Remember? We had to have a meeting with the principal."

I nod, even though I know she can't see me through

the phone. I do remember. My heart is still broken from what they've done to me. "Yes," I answer honestly. "Ally said they miss me and since we're all going away to college soon, they want to make things right. She said everything will go back to the way it was."

I hear my mom exhale deeply through the phone. "I don't know Sam. It just doesn't feel right."

My anxiety is increasing, and with my stuffy nose, I breathe heavily into the microphone. "It'll be fine," I plead. "I miss them too, mom. I already told her I forgive them and that I would love to be friends again." I pause as I try to find the right words. "I'm lonely. It would be nice to have some friends again." I feel tears well in my eyes and know I'm about to cry. "I'm so lonely, mom. I just want people to like me."

She picks up on the agony in my words as my voice begins to crack. "Awe baby, I know you do. And I want that for you, too." She poorly covers the phone as she talks to someone in the background. "I'm coming. Just give me a minute." She sighs loudly again. "OK. Tell me where you're going and who you're going with."

I wipe my eyes and snort as I attempt to clear my nasal passage. "It's the old group. Ally and Caden. And Millie, Brooke, and Brock."

"Where are you going?"

"I'm meeting them at the park at three. Ally said we're gonna hang out like old times and get to know each other again."

Once more, she sighs loudly into the phone. "And where's the party?"

"I don't know," I answer honestly. It's the truth, because I don't know. I've never been invited to a party, ever. "They send a text out an hour before, letting everyone know where it's at. Ally said that's how they keep the cops from breaking it up."

She's quiet for a moment. "I don't like it. How are you getting home? Are you drinking?"

I shake my head again, knowing full well that she can't see me. "I don't know. I might have one to fit in."

"I don't like it," she repeats. "I don't want you to get drunk. It won't mix with your medication."

"I know," I agree. I'm on anxiety medication and the doctor made it clear not to mix it with alcohol. I didn't think it'd be a problem, because I don't like alcohol, but here I am, getting invited to a party. "I don't plan to get drunk," I continue. "I just don't want to stand out if everyone else is drinking. I won't get drunk, I promise."

I hear my mother sigh again through the speaker. "Please be careful. How are you getting home?"

I shrug my shoulders. "I don't know. Probably Ally. I haven't thought about it."

"Absolutely not," she responds. "She'll most likely be drinking, and I don't want you going if you don't have a ride home." She falls silent on the other end, but only for a moment. "Why don't I come and pick you up? You text me when you're ready to come home, and I'll come get you."

"OK," I agree. I like that better.

She covers the phone again, but I'm able to hear her clearly. "I'm coming, I promise. Just one more minute." I hear her swallow as she places the phone close to her mouth. "OK. What time do you think it'll be over?"

I shrug my shoulders again. "I don't know," I answer honestly. "But everyone will probably be drunk early, I think. Maybe I should leave before then, so they don't have a chance to pick on me."

I hear silence, followed by yet another sigh. "I don't like it." Her voice trails off and I hear her cough into the phone. I hope she's not coming down with a summer cold like me. "How about eight, just to make sure nobody is mean to you when they have too much to drink? You don't know how those other boys will act at the party if they're drinking. It makes people mean. Just look at your dad."

I agree with her and I'm really nervous about going to the party. I'm nervous enough to get together with Ally and the group, but the others from my school have been awful to me over the past few years. I don't think they're just going to change overnight. "OK. I think you're right," I agree. "I'll text you when I find out where the party is."

"OK," she replies. "I just want you to be careful. Call me before you go to the party."

I nod and can't help but smile as I think about going to a party. I'm nervous about it, but I'm also excited. I'm seventeen years old and have never been to a party. This one will be my first one. "I will," I announce happily. "I love you."

"Good lord, Steve!" she barks. "I'm coming. Go on out there and I'll be right with you." Again, she sighs loudly before softening her voice for me. "OK then. I love you, and call me before you go."

We say our goodbyes and hang up before I lay my phone back on the coffee table. I pick up the remote and resume play. After turning the volume down, I stretch my arms behind my head and remember my father. I wish she hadn't brought him up. I feel anxious as fear creeps over my thoughts. He was a terrible person.

Even as a kid, I was always awkward and didn't act like the other children. Something was off with me and we didn't know what it was. He abused my mom. He was always hitting on her and calling her terrible names. It seemed like he was constantly angry and he yelled a lot. He knew I was different, but he didn't really say much to me. That is until he got drunk. When he was drinking, he'd call me 'weirdo', or 'stupid', or something else that was mean and hurtful. I'd cry, and he'd just sit back and laugh as if it was the funniest thing ever. That was back when I was Samantha. When that changed, and I transitioned, he began hitting me, too. He said that if I wanted to act like a man, he'd treat me like a man. The name calling got nastier. He referred to me as 'freak', and 'sicko', and one that hurt the worst, 'pervert'. When mom tried to protect me, he beat her badly. Put her in the hospital twice and put me next to her, only once.

The final straw was right after I turned thirteen. He came home in a fit of rage. He was belligerent drunk and tore most of the house apart. He was cussing and screaming about me and what I've done to his reputation. Apparently, some of his coworkers were laying into him about not being able to manage his household and chastising him for my actions. He fought them and lost. I think that hurt his pride, more than anything, and he beat me unmercifully for it. I can still picture the evil in his eyes and the smell of alcohol on his breath as he cussed and screamed while hitting me with blow after blow. I spent a week in the hospital with a concussion, two broken ribs, multiple contusions, and a few cuts and scrapes. The worst part of it was the permanent hearing loss that I received from it, which still affects me to this day. It'll never be right. Lost fifty percent in one ear and everything but sound in the other. He sent mom too, for getting in the middle of it. She tried to stop him and he beat her just as badly. He might have killed us if the police hadn't shown up when they did. Thank God one of the neighbors called when they heard the commotion. Otherwise, it might have been another story for me, or mom, or for both of us.

He went to jail for it and served a little over three years. We heard he got released and moved to another state, but I don't think mom cares. She just let him go and I've overheard her praying that he never comes back. I miss him sometimes though, as hard as that is to admit. He is my father and I only want his love.

I shake off the uneasiness and turn the volume back up on the television. I don't want to think about him today.

It's Friday, in the summer. I'm off of work and get to reconnect with some old friends before going to my very first party. I don't think it can get any better than this. I lay my arm over Milo and rub his head as I watch my show. I'll get a couple of episodes in, I think, before I get up and get dressed.

After I rise from the sofa, Milo leaps to the floor and trots down the hallway. As I follow, I watch him stop at the back door and glance behind him, searching for me. I open the door and stand in the doorway as he scampers a few feet before stopping to look back at me. He appears confused and doesn't understand why I hold the door open and haven't joined him yet. I don't want to go out in that sun if I don't need to.

"It's OK buddy," I say to him. "Go potty."

Hesitantly, he marches forward, into the grass and quickly relieves himself before running back to me at the door. He appears happy and looks like he wants to play. That's a rare thing for Milo, since he's not a very playful dog. He just wants to cuddle and he only wants to be near me.

Calming himself as I pull the door closed, we both enter my bedroom. He leaps to the bed and curls up next to my pillow, gazing at me while I retreat to my closet. After picking out some shorts and a light color tee shirt, I pull some socks and underwear out of my dresser before turning toward the hallway. Seeming to know that I'm going for a shower, Milo lays his head down and nestles in for another nap. What can I say? My good boy enjoys his sleep.

After undressing, I turn the water on in the shower and slide my hand through the mist. I feel the warmth of the water and immediately decide to reduce the temperature. It's still a little warm in the house and I'd rather take a cooler shower today. Maybe it'll help to cool me off. As I prepare to step inside, I catch a glimpse of myself in the mirror from the backside of the door. It's a slim mirror, designed to make a person look better than they actually do. I shudder at the sight of myself. I've never liked my body and I wish I could change it. Discarding the notion, I step under the spray and feel the cool droplets as they sting at my skin. Understanding that it'll take a minute to get used to, I stand still and cross my arms at my chest. After feeling my body slowly relax the tension, I lather up and begin to bathe.

While looking forward to this evening, I can't help but think back to my time spent with Ally. I've missed her badly and have dreamed of this day. I've lived in this house my entire life and she lives just two houses down. Our mothers were friends, and we played together, from the moment we learned to walk, until sometime during the seventh grade. That's when I transitioned. We were more than friends. We were best friends and, I thought, soul mates. We learned to ride bikes together; we learned our ABCs together, and we basically taught each other how to tie our own shoes. We were inseparable and constantly surrounded by the others. Brock and Millie are a year older than the rest of us, but they live just a few blocks away. With me, Ally, Brooke, and Caden, all starting kindergarten together and living so close to one another, the six of us became inseparable. We did everything together. We stayed at each other's houses as often as we could and we knew each other's family as well as we knew our own. I think that's pretty typical for a small midwestern town like this, and we were no exception.

We spent every minute of our spare time, up in the woods, behind the neighborhood park. There's an old dump site up there and we made a fort out of the trash people discarded. We just hung out with each other all the time. It was our special, secret hideout. Just the six of us and nobody else was allowed. I haven't been back since they shunned me in the seventh grade. Each of them grew further away from me in the years since, and all of them have picked on me at some point, except for Ally. Ally never picked on me. She just said that she wasn't allowed to hang out with me and turned her back, never to speak to me again. That broke my heart. Broke it worse than the others picking on me, as hard as that is to believe. Yeah, I definitely miss them and can't wait to hang out with them today.

After cutting off the water flow, I slide the curtain open and step out onto the rug. With no steam from the cold shower, the mirror is clear and I catch another glimpse of myself. Although I have no desire to look upon my body, I can't help but peer over its form. At seventeen, I stopped growing two years ago and ended with a height of five feet, three inches. Since I like to eat, my appetite remained the same, and I only grew wider. I'm pudgy, at a hundred and eighty pounds, but I'm working on it. If all goes well with the group today, maybe I can start getting back outside and go on some walks. That'll help. I don't like to go out around town. There's always someone who wants to make fun of me. I have brown eyes and coal black hair that I keep short. I cut it myself. I shave it up the sides, with the top kept a little longer. I think it looks pretty good, considering I don't know what I'm doing. I tried to go to a few barbershops in town, but that didn't work out. They just flat told me they didn't want to cut my hair. Said I belong in the hair salon down the street. People around here can be so mean.

Once I've dressed, I toss my clothes in the hamper near my door before walking to the kitchen. Milo immediately joins my side and takes a spot on the rug in front of the sink as I collect ingredients to make my grandma's famous oatmeal cookies. The group was always a big fan of my grandma's cookies, so I thought I'd make them a batch to take on our little get together this afternoon. Maybe that'll help ease their minds and get them to like me again. I sure hope so, and I don't think it can hurt.

Feeling invigorated by the cool shower and the

prospect of getting my friends back, I'm in high spirits and have energy that I haven't had in years. I pick up my phone and pull up my playlist. After turning the volume to max, I hit play on Drake, immediately feeling the music in my soul. Milo, sensing my enthusiasm, stares at me questioningly, but appears happy. His mouth is agape and his tongue hangs loosely from the side as he pants uncontrollably. While dancing around, I slide next to him and boop him on the nose. He immediately hunkers down and springs forward, licking at my arms as he puts his paws on my chest. I grip tightly to him and the two of us slowly dance around the kitchen floor. He hobbles around on his hind legs and appears awkward, but my dancing isn't much better. We're definitely a sight as I spin him around and he pants heavily. Although I can smell his breath, and it's awful, I ignore it to spend this glorious, happy moment with my best buddy. It's easy for me to see that he's enjoying it as much as I am, and he's probably thankful not to see me moping around the house. It's a good day.

Mixing the ingredients for the cookies is easy because I've done it a million times. My grandma never liked raisins, so she just never put them in her recipe. Most folks think it's odd, but I'm telling you, these are the best cookies ever. The secret is fresh vanilla and cornstarch. Grandma says that's what makes them so soft and chewy. After sliding the pan in the oven, I drop to the floor beneath the sink and reach for Milo as he climbs on my lap. I'm relieved when he faces his head away from me and I don't have to smell his breath. I feel bad about not being with him this evening. With so much to do today, I hate the idea of him being alone all afternoon and into tonight. Well, I guess, at least mom will be here to keep him company until I get home.

While the cookies bake, I clean the kitchen and still feel alive as the music plays in the background. My spirits couldn't be higher and I'm truly happy. I haven't felt this good in a long time but I feel it would be better if I could only smell the cookies baking. Dang cold. After I finish the dishes, I collect my phone to change to a new playlist. I feel worn out with Drake and want something different. Sliding open my phone, I catch a glimpse of my Instagram app and consider opening it and restarting my account. I had to pause it last year when the bullying got too severe and I haven't had it since. I've considered starting a fake account to keep tabs on my schoolmates, but I don't really know how to make it work. I fear it would be suspect and they'd catch me, only to make things worse. After clicking on the app, I quickly reconsider and close it out. I'll wait and see how today goes. If I think I've gotten my friends back, then I'll restart my account.

When the timer sounds for the oven, I open the door and peer inside. Lightly golden and perfect. I pull the pan from the oven and place it on the counter to cool. While I wait, I jog down the hall to my bedroom to retrieve my wallet and house keys. It's getting close to time for me to go to grandma's and I don't want to be late. As I turn back into the hallway, I find Milo sitting at the back door, staring at me.

"Do you need to go out, buddy?" I ask.

Milo spins in a circle and puts his nose against the door. I laugh to myself as I step closer and open the door. Following closely behind him, I again walk into the backyard. It's hot and humid outside. Almost immediately, beads of sweat form on my forehead, and I'm shaken by the sheer heat of the sun as it beams down from above. Still, not a cloud in sight. As Milo finishes quickly and sprints back to my side, I feel relieved that he's chosen to do his business fast today. He usually takes forever while he hunts for the perfect spot. It must be the heat and I don't think he likes it either. Maybe I'll choose a college up north, so it's not as hot for the two of us.

I lock the back door and make my way to the kitchen. While removing the cookies from the pan, I stack them neatly on one of my mother's good china platters and fight the urge to sample one. Although I can't really smell them, my memory does, and I want nothing more than to devour one, or maybe six, of them. Winning my third calorie battle of the day, I refrain and choose to wait and eat them with my friends. I walk to the living room with Milo right on my heels and open the front door. He sits comfortably on the carpet as I rub his head. "I'll be back in a little while," I tell him as I pull the door closed behind me and step out onto the front porch.

It's just as hot out front as it is in the back, and I feel the sun's eternal power as I scoot down our stairs to the sidewalk. On my walk to grandma's house, the heat radiates from the concrete and I feel sweat popping out on my forehead and running down my face. It's beading up on my hairline and trailing down the nape of my neck, moistening my shirt as I walk. Luckily, grandma's house is only a few blocks away, and I feel gassed as I cross her lawn. My nose is running and I struggle to breathe through all the stuffiness. I can feel my hot breath as I pant open mouthed, without the ability to take any air through my nose. I'm short of breath as I open her door and step inside.

The coolness of her house is glorious and I wish our air worked as well as hers. Before I'm able to announce myself, I hear her in the kitchen as she cooks away, and I don't think she heard me enter. I quietly kick my shoes off at the door and tiptoe toward the sound she creates. I feel joyous when I see her bent over, with her back facing me, and I know I need to get her. I slow my creep, hoping to scare her as I inch my way closer. She's muttering something to herself, but I can't quite make out what she says. A smile is halfway across my face as I anticipate the fright that I'm about to give to her. Just when I get within five feet, she turns toward me. Caught by surprise, she jumps and throws a towel in the air as she leaps backward.

"Dammit, Sammy," she calls out while bending over and clutching at her chest. "Do you want to give me a heart attack?"

I rush to her side, unable to control my laughter. "I'm sorry, grandma. I just had to do it."

Grandma leans sideways and picks up the towel. As she stands upright, she swings it and hits me on the arm. "Asshole!" she exclaims while wrapping me in a hug. "You could've killed me."

Still laughing, I embrace her back and feel the warmth of her hug. I don't know what I'd do without my grandma. She's my rock and has supported me through everything.

"Sit down and behave," she continues as we release. She points to a chair at the table. "Lunch will be ready soon."

I take a seat and scoop a magazine from the table. I shake my head and can't believe that she still gets People magazine. While I continue smiling at the memory of scaring her, I thumb through the pages before quickly placing it back on the table. I have no interest in reading about today's celebrities. They're all self-absorbed and only care about themselves. I turn my chair to face her while she works at the stove and I watch her stir away at a pot. Her chubby body jiggles as she stirs, and I smile at the sight of her. Must be where I get my body type from, I think.

Grandma Dorothy is a short and chunky bullish woman that stands barely over five feet. She cusses like a sailor and drinks like a fish. She's never been short of sharing her thoughts, whether it hurts your feelings or not. I'm pretty sure the only people that like her, other than mom and me, are her girlfriends. My grandpa drowned in a boating accident when I was a baby, so I never met him and grandma never remarried. Mom says he was very calm and collected, which is why he and grandma worked so well. Grandma has always been there for me. She supports me in the decisions I make and defends me when she thinks others do me wrong. Mom and I almost had to tackle her to keep her from going to the school when the kids were bullying me real bad. I thought she was going to kill someone. She loves me with all her heart and I feel the same way about her.

"What're we having?" I ask

"Potato soup."

"Potato soup?" I question. "Grandma, it's a hundred degrees outside."

She stops stirring and turns back toward me. "So what? It's never too hot for soup. That's just a state of mind." She scoffs and turns back to the stove before continuing. "It's not a hundred degrees in here, is it?"

I shake my head and can't help but think that she's not wrong. It is cold in here and I'm once again reminded of her fantastic air conditioning. "Still," I reply. "I don't think it's normal for people to eat potato soup in the middle of summer."

Again, grandma scoffs as she turns back to face me. "Good thing we're not normal. I guess we couldn't eat this delicious soup if we were like everyone else."

I smile after catching her point. She and I are definitely not normal. I'm more different than she is, but my dear grandmother is a nut in her own right. She marches to the beat of a different drum and I love her for it. And, her soup is always delicious.

"You're right," I concede. "Good thing we're not normal."

Grandma smiles back at me as she cuts off the flame from the stove and I watch her retreat to the cabinet for bowls. After returning to the stove, she ladles the soup into them and I watch the steam wisp from the top as she walks them to the table. She places one in front of me and one to the side before taking a seat next to me.

"I forgot the spoons," she states as she shakes her head. "Give me a minute to get them."

"That's OK, grandma," I reply while standing to my feet. "I'll get them."

She smiles as I rise and make my way across the kitchen before returning with two spoons. After passing her one, I sit down when she speaks up. "Aren't you a dear. Why don't you go ahead and get us a couple of Cokes out of the fridge while you're up."

I nod and cross the floor to the refrigerator for two Cokes, before once again returning to the table. They're actually Diet Cokes, but I don't think I'll mention it.

"Dammit," she calls out as I return. "Do you mind grabbing the parmesan out of the door of the fridge? I like parmesan cheese in my soup."

I again nod and return to the fridge, pulling the parmesan bottle out and carrying it to my grandma. I set it on the table in front of her and sit down.

"Will you?"

I glance up at her to see what else she needs, only to see her grinning from ear to ear.

"Sit down," she laughs. "I'm only kidding. I don't need anything else."

I laugh with her as I take a seat, and we have lunch. Although my taste is not what it usually is, because of this cold, the soup is fantastic and she was right. It's never too hot to have soup and I like it so much that I refill my bowl for a second helping. We discuss things that've been going on in each of our lives, and there's not much to report on either side. I stay home and work at the diner, and she frequents the casino or plays bingo with her buddies. My grandma is a drinker, and she and her gal pals like to go to the casino to drink it up. They never use an Uber. They take turns making one of their kids or grandkids drive them to and from the casino. I've done it twice, since I got my license, and I enjoy listening to them on the way home when they're all liquored up. They like to sing old country songs and they crank the music as loud as they can. I'm not sure if it's because they're hard of hearing, or if they just like it loud. I can tell you one thing, though, not a single one of them can carry a tune. They're enjoyable, but awful.

"Do you want to come over tonight and watch television?" she asks after we finish and I put my bowl in the sink.

"I can't," I admit while slipping her a sheepish grin. "I'm meeting Ally and the others. We're all going to a party."

As grandma stands to her feet, her smile opens wide, and she places her hand on my arm. "Oh, how nice," she replies. "I hope you have a good time." She walks her bowl to the sink and turns back toward me. "How is Ally?"

"I don't know," I answer honestly. "Haven't really talked to her very much. We're just reconnecting today."

She gives me a wink and wraps her arms around me. "That's nice," she says. "I'm glad you two are going to finally work things out."

I smile back at her as I turn on the faucet to wash the dishes. Just as quickly as I turned it on, she shuts it off. "Don't even think about it," she grumbles.

"But grandma," I return. "You cooked. I'll wash the dishes."

"Not a chance," she replies. "It'll give me something to do later. What's an old woman to do when she has no one around?"

"It's Friday," I answer. "Why don't you go to the casino?"

She shakes her head and purses her lips. "Can't. We went last night and them ole birds can't handle two nights out. I need to get some younger friends so they can keep up with me."

Both of us laugh as we exit the kitchen. Grandma plops down in her recliner as I retreat to the door and begin putting on my shoes. "Where are you going?" she asks. "You just got here."

I nod and sigh aloud. "Yeah, but I have a couple of places to stop before I go meet everyone. I better get going. I don't want to be late."

She rises from the recliner. "Do you want to take my car? It'll be faster."

I shake my head, even though I'd love to use her car. "I'll just walk. It's not that far and I can use the exercise." I pat at my belly. "I want to lose a couple of pounds before I go back to school and the two bowls of soup I ate aren't going to help."

Grandma chuckles as she makes her way to me for another hug. "I think you look just fine," she replies while squeezing me tightly. "You have a good time tonight. You deserve it."

I smile as I open the door and step out onto the porch. "Just remember," she continues. "Don't do anything I wouldn't do, but if you do, grandma will bail you out."

I chuckle aloud as she delivers a boisterous laugh and closes the door behind me. As I stand on the porch, I think I can still hear her laughing from inside and wonder if she thought it was actually that funny. I shake my head and descend the steps, once again placing my feet on the fiery sidewalk.

The walk to the diner is a long and hot one. I'm disappointed in myself for not borrowing grandma's car. It would've been cooler and I could've gotten there much quicker. I could've finished everything I needed to do and spent more quality time with Milo before meeting the guys. As I walk and nearly suffocate, I turn my thoughts to the get together tonight. Of course, I'm excited to see Ally most of all, but I miss the others too. A couple of years after I transitioned, and they stopped being my friends, Ally started dating Caden. Caden and I always got along well. He has a personality that just attracts you to him and although, not anymore, I was a lot like him and Brock. We were all athletes, so it just seemed to work. From kindergarten on, we played every type of sport and hung out, even outside of the group. When we were all together, Caden and I would gravitate to each other. We were always in competition with one another. Who could do the most chin ups? Who could run the fastest or throw the farthest? I always got the best of him. That is, up until the year before I changed. His body caught up, and he exceeded me in everything. He's the best athlete in school, and by far, the most popular. Everyone likes him and why shouldn't they? He's funny, and kind, and really good looking. Ally didn't bully me, but neither did Caden, really. He just made some off handed comments about me in front of his friends that I overheard. I'm not sure if he even knows that I heard him. I bet he would be devastated if he knew how much I cried when hearing his words. It hurt me to lose him as a dear friend.

As I enter the diner, I notice how busy it is and worry that I'll interrupt their service by asking for my new uniforms. Maybe I should wait and pick them up next week. I shake it off. Since I'm here, I might as well get them. I step to the counter and wait patiently as my boss Tom rings up a customer while they prepare to leave. He glances up and sees me, so I smile at him. He doesn't acknowledge me as he exchanges their change and I step to the side as the couple walks past me to the door. Tom turns on his heels and disappears to the kitchen. I assume he's gone to the office for my uniforms, so I wait patiently.

As I wait, I scan the room. Growing up in this town, I recognize most people in here. Some I know by name, but most just in passing. I feel uncomfortable when I catch a few of them gawking at me and a couple in the back point at me while they whisper. I know what they think and it hurts every single time. I don't know why it's such a big deal for everyone around here. I wish they'd just let me be.

"Excuse me, miss."

I turn to see Millie's father as he nods toward the restroom. I've known him my entire life. Millie was one of my best friends and he watched me grow up. I guess he forgot. I notice that I unknowingly block the walkway and immediately feel ashamed. "I'm sorry," I reply as I step to the side and allow him room to pass.

As he walks by, he scoffs in my direction, but says nothing else. I feel my face go flush with embarrassment and I step closer to the counter, hoping Tom returns quickly. That's why I changed my name to Sammy. It was just too hard for everyone to go from Samantha to Sam, so I compromised. I can't wait to get out of this place and move on to a more accepting community. It really hurt my feelings, the way he just looked at me. There was a time that I loved that man. It's not usually this bad when I'm here at work. I'm not nearly as uncomfortable. I'm able to stay in the back, either cooking or washing dishes. Sure, Tom and the other manager are rude to me, and most of the workers won't talk to me, but it goes OK. When it gets slow, there's always something that needs cleaned, and I can bury myself back there, with no need to see the customers or interact with the other workers. I'm a good worker, I think.

Finally, Tom steps through the doors but doesn't glance in my direction. He walks from behind the counter and makes his way to the customers. I watch as he goes from person to person, chatting and patting them on the shoulder. My nose is running, so I step behind the counter for a napkin.

Noticing my movement, Tom glances up from his conversation and makes a beeline for me. He appears angry as he walks briskly in my direction. Just as I retrieve a napkin and wait for his arrival, he steps directly in front of me.

"What do you think you're doing?" he barks.

Taken aback, I can only stare blankly at him as I wipe my nose. "I just needed a tissue," I answer.

He narrows his gaze at me. "You're not allowed to be behind the counter when you're not working," he states. "We don't want to risk anyone stealing."

I've known Tom for a long time. Prior to working here, we frequented this diner when I was a kid. There are only a couple of fast-food places, this diner, and a Mexican restaurant to eat in this town, and this was our favorite spot. He's worked here for over twenty years and has known me forever.

"I'm sorry, Tom," I respond and hate that I'm bothering him. "I didn't mean to get in the way."

He glares his eyes at me and shakes his head in disgust. "What do you want?"

Again, taken aback by his demeanor, I sheepishly reply. "I, uh. I need to pick up my uniforms."

Tom sneers and looks me up and down. "You mean shirts?" he asks. "We're just giving you shirts. You're only part time and you'll be required to buy your own pants."

I nod, understanding what he means. "Yes. I'm here for my shirts."

He lifts his head but glares his eyes down at me while he smirks and points beyond the counter. "Wait out there and I'll get them."

I step from behind the counter and start to speak as he turns on his heels and once again disappears into the kitchen. I feel my cheeks are flush as I patiently stand, waiting for him to return. I sense the others staring at me behind my back. His voice was loud enough to draw attention to us and I feel their eyes on me.

To my satisfaction, he quickly returns and plops down a stack of tee shirts on the counter. "I'll see you Sunday," he mutters as he turns and storms off.

"Tom," I call out. "Can I get a bag? I walked here and don't have any way to carry them."

He steps back to the counter and leans close as he lowers his voice. "We're not wasting a bag on an employee. That's your problem. Deal with it."

Feeling uncomfortable, I pick up the stack of shirts and turn away. For whatever reason, I glance at the tag on one shirt and notice that it's an extra-large. After placing them back on the counter, I thumb through each of them to find they all read the same size. I look up to find him staring down the edge of his nose at me.

"Tom," I speak calmly. "These are extra-large and I wear an extra, extra-large. I think you gave me the wrong ones."

A devilish grin crosses his face as he speaks. "That's what you ordered, so that's what you get."

I shake my head. I know I ordered the right size. I know my size and would never order something different. Especially something smaller. "Tom," I plead. "These won't fit. I can't wear them."

Still grinning, Tom stares straight into my eyes. "Lose some weight and maybe they'll fit you."

My mouth falls open and I'm unable to speak as he simply chuckles to himself and disappears back into the kitchen. My cheeks burn with embarrassment as I stand there, staring at the swinging door. Feeling uneasy, I collect the shirts and stuff them under my arm before turning toward the door and exiting.

Back on the sidewalk, the heat again stings my skin. Already running hot from my interaction with Tom, I feel as if I'm going to melt. I put my head down and walk toward the end of the street. The shirts are bulky and I'm thankful that I don't have far to go until I reach the pharmacy. At least I will get a bag with the purchase of my medicine, I think.

Our small town is compact. The housing is tightly constructed, surrounded by large farms and woods. We have a main highway leading into the city limits with a few businesses, restaurants, and convenient stores. But the center of town offers everything a person can need. Right in the middle of town, is our town square. In the middle of that square, is a beautiful old courthouse with room for our police station, city hall, and clerk's offices. Surrounding it on all four sides are all the businesses that make this town function. The diner that I work in is on the north side of the square, and the pharmacy is less than a block away, on the west side of the square, near the corner.

The walk to the pharmacy is quick, and I hear the bell ding as I enter. I always loved that sound and wonder how old the bell is. To my right is a checkout counter and I recognize the girl working the register. She is a year younger than me, and fairly popular. After nodding my head at her, I see her snarl at me and put her head down as she continues playing on her phone. Not wanting to ask her for anything, I continue toward the back and scan the aisles as I search for decongestants. Unable to locate them, I have no option but to approach the counter and ask for help. Just as I arrive, I hear the bell ring out, and turn to see our new police chief. I don't know her name, but I think it's pretty cool that we have a female as chief. She nods at me and steps in line behind me at the counter. I reciprocate with a smile, just as the cashier glances up at me from her phone.

Feeling the sweat on my arm from carrying the stack of shirts, I place them on the counter and watch as she gives a disgusted look before blinking slowly at me.

"Um, hi," I begin. "I can't find the decongestants. Can you point me in the direction?"

Again, she snarls at me. "They're back here," she grumbles. "We can't leave them out for people to make meth with." She glances at the police chief and smiles as if she's proud of herself.

I nod my head and smile politely. "May I have a box, please?"

"Are you gonna make meth with them?" she questions, while narrowing her eyes at me.

"Uh, I don't believe so," I joke and let out a little laugh. "I don't know how?"

Again, she simply snarls as she turns behind the counter to collect the box of decongestants and I smile sheepishly at the chief. She gives me a smile in return, but I think she looks a little sidetracked as she glances down at her phone and begins typing.

"Is that it?"

I turn back to her and nod. "That's it."

Her mouth opens with a devilish grin. "You sure? You don't need some puberty blockers. Maybe some testosterone?" She laughs. "How about some tampons?"

The smile disappears from my face and feel it turn red with embarrassment. "No thank you," I answer as I place my debit card on the counter. "Just the medicine."

Still feeling proud of herself, she smiles broadly and points at the wall behind me. "You sure? The tampons are just right over there."

Not knowing what to say, I attempt to form words as a voice speaks up behind me. Although it's definitely female, it has a sharpness to it. "That's enough. Just ring him up."

Completely embarrassed, I keep my head down as she snatches my card and completes the transaction. She stuffs the decongestant in a small paper bag and tosses it on the counter.

"Have a good day," she mutters.

I glance up and immediately dread what I'm about to ask. "I'm so sorry," I say. "But can I get a plastic bag so I can put my shirts in there?"

She scoffs at me. "No," she answers coldly. "That's not our problem. You can carry them out, just the way you carried them in."

"Just give him a bag! Now!"

I turn toward the chief and see she is staring intently at the cashier. As her eyes turn toward me, she gives me a little wink, and although I'm completely ashamed, I can't help but smile.

"Thank you," I mouth silently as the cashier tosses a plastic bag on the counter and stares blankly at me.

I quickly stuff the decongestant and the shirts in the bag, fumbling through my nervousness. I put my head down and walk to the door. "Thank you," I say aloud as I open it. The bell rings out, and I again smile at its sound before stepping outside into the blistering sunlight. People can be so mean.

Standing on the sidewalk, I exhale heavily through my mouth and snort my clogged nose as I try to wash away the humiliation. Although the chief was nice and took up for me, I really wish she didn't have to see that. I don't like the fact that our first encounter was one where she saw me so weak. One day, I'm going to speak up for myself.

The nursing home is eight blocks from here, nestled tightly within a housing neighborhood. As I begin along the sidewalk, I take a moment to notice the beauty of our town square. Everything is perfectly clean. The trees are neatly maintained, and although it's summer, the grass is bright green. Each shop displays some form of our team mascot. Football is big around here and Caden is our star quarterback, but another member of the group, Brock, is a star in his own right. He is our running back, and he's going into his senior season. Although he no longer speaks to me,

I heard that he's already signed with a college. I'm proud of him for his accomplishment, even though he's been mean to me directly.

Brock is most like me out of our old group. He's a top-notch athlete, like Caden, so I competed heavily against him too. He grew up poor and also had an alcoholic father. We shared a connection growing up, and it made us really close, even though we never spoke about it. I think we were both relieved, just to have someone around that we could relate to. All the others come from a tight-knit family, so they couldn't understand. It's hard to comprehend how a father beats his child, but I saw it happen to my mother and mourned for Brock when I found out that he had also been abused. I wonder now if he ever heard what my father did to me and that we now have that in common. Did he cry for me, just as I did for him?

Even as a kid, he worried about everything and always thought something bad was going to happen. I know he probably felt terrible about being mean to me and I forgive him for it. I understand how hard he had to work to fit in at school because he was so poor and an outcast, so I get it. I remember that he never had good shoes, and in the sixth grade, my grandma bought him a new pair for school. I always liked that about her and I can remember him crying and hugging her tightly when she gave them to him. He's a year older than me, but we were close. I think we leaned on each other since neither of us had any money and the others did. I miss him and look forward to speaking with him. I just hope he doesn't bring my mood down with his negativity. I'm feeling pretty good today.

Located directly beside the nursing home is a daycare with children running around the playground. Feeling the sweatiness on my palm from carrying the bag, I switch hands and notice that it actually feels good. My hand was aching, but I hadn't noticed until now. As I walk along the fence, I stop for a moment and rest my elbows on the railing as I watch the children at play. I watch joyfully as a ball rolls next to where I stand, and a little boy, maybe five or six years old, runs up to the fence and picks it up. Staring up at me, he smiles and lifts it over his head as he offers it to me.

"You want me to throw it?" I ask and return his smile. Happily, I reach out to take the ball from him.

As he nods, a young lady jerks the ball from his hand and glares at me through her glasses. She stuffs the ball under her arm and grabs him by the hand, leading him away.

"Come on Jacob," she snaps. "We don't play with those people."

My mouth falls open and I shake my head as I watch her drag him away, only to glance back at me over her shoulder, snarling as she goes. What the hell did I do to her, I wonder?

She leads him back to the building and stands next to a slightly older lady. The two of them are mouthing something to one another and watching me intently. Neither breaks their stare, and each is equally discomforting.

Not wanting to cause any problems, I turn toward the nursing home and pick up my pace as I cross the parking lot. I'm looking forward to my time at the nursing home. I'm not employed by them and they don't pay me, but it is rewarding. They treat me good and I like to spend the time with the older people. I usually help clean or restock supplies, but I always find time to chat with someone. It's one of the few places I can go in town without being judged. You'd think the older folks would be meaner to me, but they're not. It's the middle-aged people and the ones closer to my age. Sure, I've had a few issues with some of the staff and a couple of residents, but it's easy to stay away from those individuals. There's always something to do. And like I said, they treat me pretty well, overall.

As I walk in the door, I'm greeted by the director, Maria. She's an older Hispanic woman who treats me very well. I like Maria.

"Hola, Sam."

She smiles and I don't have to force one in return, since my face displays my happiness to see her. "Hola, Mrs. Sanchez," I reply confidently. She's been teaching me Spanish while I've been helping around here and I hope to get it down, eventually.

"No, no, no," she corrects while waggling her finger back and forth. "Senora Sanchez."

"Sorry, Senora Sanchez," I repeat and feel disappointed in my ability to roll my R's. I've been practicing, but it appears I still need some work. "What do you need me to do today?"

She continues smiling and pats me on the back as she leads me to through the door into the lounge. There are at least ten elders milling about, and all appear to be having a good time. They're busy playing games, visiting with one another, or simply watching television. I hear the chatter and laughter within the room and feed from it. As odd as it sounds, this is a happy place for me.

"Easy day, today," she answers. "You can play games or visit with them. It's up to you. We don't have anything pressing today."

That makes me happy because I'm not able to stay long. I need to make sure I don't miss our hang out this afternoon and I don't want to be late.

"I think I'll play some games," I say as I scan the room, searching for Barbara. She's my favorite and I've grown really attached to her. Not able to spot her, I turn back to Maria. "Where's Barb?"

Maria pouts her lip and shakes her head. "She

didn't want to come out. She said she doesn't feel well."

I mimic her and pout my lip upon hearing the news. I like Barbara. "That sucks," I respond. "I wish I could see her and hope she feels better soon."

"Go ahead," she replies. "She's in her room and it might do her some good to have your company. Her family hasn't been to see her in weeks."

I shake my head in disappointment, but feel good after getting her permission to see Barbara. I really like her. "You sure you don't need my help cleaning?"

She shakes her head. "No," she answers. "We had a boy that was on probation and got assigned to help out." She grins widely. "We worked his butt off and made him clean everything."

I laugh as I offer a fist bump and move down the hall toward Barbara's room. Not only do I enjoy her company, she is the grandma of one of my old friends from the group, Brooke. Our history goes back to before kindergarten and we used to go to Barbara's house when we were kids. She was always so loving and kind to us. She gave us cookies and milk and played with us in the backyard. I could always tell they had money, but they never acted like it. They dressed well and had nice things, but were really down to earth. Brooke's mom and dad worked all the time, and that's how I got to know Barbara so well. Brooke was always there and Barbara had no problem letting the six of us kids run around her place. She's awesome and Brooke is a lot like her. She always thinks of others and goes out of her way to help people.

When we were little, both of us wanted to be veterinarians. We each loved dogs, and cats, and just about every animal you can think of. Maybe not snakes, though. Who likes snakes? I was completely shocked when she stopped talking to me and heartbroken when I saw her comment on an Instagram post, making fun of me. I don't know if she knew I could see it, but it hurt me badly to think that she could say something like that about me behind my back. Although that was tough, it was nothing compared to what she told me in private. She told me, point blank, that I was a sinner and going to hell. Brooke is a devout Christian and doesn't stray from her beliefs for anyone, even me. It tore me apart to lose her. Especially after growing up together and our long friendship. I miss Brooke and can't wait to see her.

"Hello Barb," I announce as I stick my head through the door.

She immediately opens with a smile. "Hello Sammy," she replies. "I'm glad you're here."

I walk into the room and watch as she scoots a little higher on her bed, almost sitting up. I can see that she's still in her nightgown as she pulls the blanket up to her chest.

"Sit down," she continues, while pointing at a recliner across the room. "What have you been up to today?"

I plop down in the chair before answering. "Had to get my new uniforms," I say while holding up the bag. "And I had to go to the pharmacy to get cold medicine." I suck and blow with my nose, trying to let her hear how stuffy I am. "Mom says I have a summer cold."

"Oh dear," she replies and appears to be worried. "Well, I hope you feel better soon."

I notice the television is on, but there's no sound coming from it. "I hear you're not feeling very well today, either."

She shakes her head. "I'm not sick," she corrects me. "I miss my family and they haven't been by to see me. I'm just lonely."

Hearing her say it out loud makes me feel bad for her. I see the sadness in her eyes and I hate it. Everyone deserves to have family visit them. Especially when you raised them. "They're probably busy," I say in hoping to make her feel better. "You know they're always working."

She gives me a smile and nods her head. "You're probably right, and having you here now makes me happy. Have you seen Brooke?"

I shake my head. "Not lately," I lie. "She's been too busy, and I've been working every day. We just haven't had the time."

I've never told Barb that Brooke and I are no longer friends. I think it would devastate her and I don't want her to be disappointed in Brooke for shunning me. In the off chance that she agrees with Brooke, I don't want to lose her as a friend, either. Friends are tough to come by for me, and I'll even take the old ones.

Barbara and I go back and forth, exchanging pleasantries, before we finally agree to play some cards. I set up a TV tray next to her bed and slide the recliner close. It's pretty difficult for me to move it, since it's a big recliner, and I feel the weakness in my arms. I need to work out. I'm not very strong and I have no hopes of getting any stronger without the gym.

We play cards for over an hour while Barbara tells me stories about her childhood and her marriage to her husband. She's an excellent conversationalist and I fall in love with her stories from the years past. I like history, and she describes everything in such great detail that I'm able to imagine everything she tells me about. I'm happy that she's so good with conversation, because I'm not. I haven't had a lot of practice and it's nice to have someone else to carry the bulk of the load. Sure, I give feedback and make small comments, but that's about it. I just aid in the storyline to keep it going.

After looking at the clock on the wall, I notice it's getting late and I don't want to miss the guys this afternoon. I'm looking forward to seeing them all and can't wait.

"Well, Barbara," I state as I find a point in her story

to make my exit. "I need to go. I have some friends to catch up with, and I don't want to be late."

"No, you don't," she replies. "Nobody wants to be around someone that's late. It's an irritation."

I nod in agreement, although I'm not sure if it's completely true. I slide the recliner back to its place and stack up the deck of cards. "Do you need anything before I go?" I ask.

She nods her head and smiles as I fold the table and turn to face her. "Just a hug," she answers.

My face can't hide my happiness at her request, but it quickly fades when I think of the consequences. "I can't," I admit. "I'm sick and I don't want to get you sick."

She continues smiling and stretches her arms out. "That's just bull crap," she replies. "You can't catch a summer cold from a hug. That's not how it works."

I chuckle aloud, not knowing if she's right or wrong, before leaning down to give her a hug. I hold my breath, hoping not to spread any germs on her as she squeezes me tightly and rubs small circles on my back. She holds me so long that I feel lightheaded and as if I'm going to pass out. Finally, she releases me and I exhale slowly, trying not to let her see that I was holding my breath.

"Thank you," I mutter and notice that I sound winded. "I'll see you soon."

She tells me goodbye as I exit the room and begin down the hallway. Feeling empty handed, I remember my bag and turn around. As I reenter her room, I see her climbing out of bed. Almost immediately, I notice her legs. They're so skinny and I can see her bones as the skin hangs loosely. She appears malnourished

She sees me in the doorway and points next to the recliner while grinning. "You forgot your bag, honey," she states. "I thought I was going to have to chase you down."

I give her a courtesy chuckle and scoop up my bag

as I turn back toward the door. "Thank you," I reply. "You probably could've caught me as fast as you are."

I hear Barbara laughing as I leave her room and continue down the hall. I'm worried about her. She appears so frail and so sickly. How have I not noticed that before? I'll definitely tell Brooke that she needs to check on her grandma when I see her later. Surely, she'll want to know.

As I enter the lounge, I notice most of the people have gone back to their rooms and only a few remain. I give them a wave as I pass through to the lobby, and each of them greets me in return. I don't see Maria anywhere and it makes me feel sad not to say goodbye. Figuring that she's probably busy, and not wanting to disturb her, I continue through the door and step outside.

Again, the heat radiates from the sidewalk and intensifies as I walk across the parking lot. I don't know why the asphalt seems hotter than the concrete, but I figure it must have something to do with the color. The sun beams down from above and there's still not a cloud in the sky. It would be nice to have some wind, on a day like today, but there's not an ounce of breeze blowing anywhere.

After taking to the sidewalk, I feel the sweat running down my back and collecting in my crack. I'm breathing heavily and my stuffiness hasn't reduced a bit. I'm so uncomfortable and I hate the idea of meeting the group when I feel like this. It would be perfect if I could just stay home with Milo and watch Game of Thrones all evening. But I can't. I need to see the guys and catch up with them. Nothing would make me happier than to make up with them and have them back in my life.

A couple of blocks from the nursing home, I pass by another house where I used to play when I was young. That's where Millie used to live, and I wonder if she still does. I spot the top of a swing set in the backyard and recognize it from when we were kids. Ally fell off the slide when we were ten and broke her collarbone. I thought it was the most gruesome thing in the world and worried that Ally would die. I cried all night and wouldn't listen to my mom when she assured me she'd be fine and was definitely going to survive. It was very traumatizing for me back then and I laugh at the thought of it now.

Millie and I were good buddies back in the day. I wouldn't say we were the best of friends and I don't remember being at her house without one of the others, but we liked each other. She was the meanest to me after I transitioned. She was more focused on maintaining her social status than on continuing our friendship. She refused to hear me out and has trashed me since then. She has openly made fun of me in school, but never smiles when doing it, which I find to be odd. She just looks at me like I'm a piece of garbage. I miss her too, as odd as it sounds. She was my friend and I love her. We had a lot of good times together. She might be the hardest one for me to forgive, but I will, eventually. I'm just going to need some time.

As I arrive back at my house, my shirt is drenched with sweat and I pull it off as soon as I close the door behind me. I hear Milo jump to the floor and meet him in the hallway as I near my bedroom. Using the sweaty tee shirt, I wipe my chest and back before drying my armpits. I toss the bag on my bed, and the sweaty shirt in the hamper before grabbing another one from the closet. This time, I go with plain white. I hope it helps with this heat and I'll take any reduction in temperature that I can get.

While turning from the closet, I feel Milo's nose pressed firmly against my thigh. I kneel to his side and caress his body while he tries to lick my face. Catching a whiff of his breath, I pull back but feel guilty, so I hug him tightly and rub at his belly. I hate being so distant with him because of his rotten breath. I need to get him to the vet soon, so that I can love him like he deserves.

"You need to go out, buddy?" I ask after standing to my feet.

Showcasing his happiness, he spins in circles as his tongue hangs limply from the side of his mouth. He leaps backward and turns toward the hallway, glancing back and waiting for me to join. As I step close to him, he jumps in the air and darts out of the room. After turning in the hallway, I see him with his nose pressed firmly against the door. I can't help but laugh at the way he answers my question, and I believe he does, in fact, need to go out.

After opening the door, I watch from the doorway as he bounds down the stairs and stops short of the grass. Peering back at me with his big dark eyes, he waits for me to join and I feel bad about not wanting to brave the heat with him. I know he wants me by his side, but I just can't do it. I've been out in it long enough and I'll soon be with the others at the fort and unable to get any air. I really need the cold, if only for a few minutes.

"Sorry buddy," I speak to him. "You're on your own. Go pee pee."

Seeming to understand, he circles the yard twice before squatting down to relieve himself. My mom finds it odd that he squats and never lifts his leg like other dogs, but it doesn't bother me. He should be able to pee however he likes.

When he finishes, he turns and darts in my direction. I open the door as he bursts through and spins in circles a few times. All at once, he raises on his hind legs and puts his paws on my chest. I giggle and ruffle his head while he licks away at my arms. Content with my affection, he drops to the floor and shuffles off to the kitchen. I hear him drinking from his water bowl as I duck in the bathroom. Quickly, I wash the stinky residue left by his tongue from my hands and arms before drying them. I pull off a large portion of toilet paper and attempt to blow my nose.

Momentarily, my nostrils clear before quickly plugging back over and I shake my head with the discomfort that it causes me on this very important day.

I duck back in my bedroom and empty the contents of the bag onto my bed. I pick up one of my new shirts and hold it up to my body. There is no way I can fit in this shirt and I have no idea what I'm going to do to get one that fits. I guess I'll have to ask the other manager at the diner, but he treats me about the same as Tom. They're just not very nice men.

I drop the shirt back on my bed and grab the box of decongestant. As I walk down the hall toward the kitchen, I read the back of the box. I notice immediately that a potential side effect is drowsiness. Not wanting to risk the medication in disrupting my fun this evening, I toss it on the counter. I'll take it tonight when I get home. It won't hurt anything, and it's just a few hours delayed.

Feeling completely dehydrated, I pull a bottle of water out of the refrigerator and take a long drink. The cold water is refreshing, but it stings as it goes down my throat. I take a breath, huffing and puffing from not being able to breathe through my nose while I drink. After two more gulps, I finish the entire bottle and toss it in the trash before grabbing another one. I remove the lid and take only a sip before I notice Milo's water bowl is empty. I set the bottle on the counter and pick up his bowl. He gets happy and spins in circles as I refill it at the sink. While I wait, I take another sip of my water and put the lid back on.

Once Milo's water bowl is full, I put the cookies in a freezer bag and feel the anticipation rise within me as it nears the time for me to meet with the group. I'm so nervous and hope everything goes well. I place the cookies on the counter next to my water bottle and jog down the hallway to the bathroom. After glancing in the mirror and noticing salt streaks on my forehead from a full day of sweat, I pull my shirt off and splash water on my face. I take the time to lightly rinse my hair before toweling off and putting my shirt back on. Reaching out, I grab a bottle from the shelf and spray a few mists of cologne across my body to ensure I smell as good as possible. After all, this is a second, first impression.

Returning to the kitchen, I grab the bottle of water and the bag of cookies before turning to the door. I notice Milo sitting by his food bowl, gazing at me. Catching my eyesight, he paws at his bowl and whines softly, showing his desire to be fed. I chuckle aloud at the sight of my beloved buddy as he begs to eat. Feeling that it's too early, I pet his head.

"Sorry buddy," I speak to him with a childish voice. "Mom will feed you when she gets home. It's too early for dinner."

He continues pawing at his bowl, but I ignore him as I retreat to the living room. I don't want to be late. As I turn to pull the door closed behind me, I see him sitting on the floor, staring at me, and I sense sadness in him.

"I'll be back soon," I express as I close the door and lock it from the outside.

The first thing I notice when I step on the sidewalk is the excruciating temperature. The sun seems brighter and the heat feels as if I'm walking through fire. After only a few steps along the concreted sidewalk, I feel the soles of my shoes warming, so I step to the grass. I transfer the water bottle to my back pocket and use my free hand to fish my phone out of my pocket. Since it's now the hottest part of the day, I'm curious what the temperature is, and if we've actually reached the record. After opening the weather app, I'm surprised to see that it's only a hundred and twelve degrees. There's still quite a bit to go before we hit the record, but being that it's the Midwest, the humidity is the killer.

"Get off my grass!"

Startled, I glance up to see Ally's father at the mailbox on their porch. I immediately jump back to the sidewalk and wave at him. "Sorry Mr. Carpenter," I apologize. "My feet were getting hot from the concrete."

His stares burn holes into my soul as he watches me with absolute contempt. "I don't care," he yells back. "Stay out of my yard!"

My cheeks are already red and warm from the heat, but I still feel it go flush with embarrassment. I offer another apology, but he briskly retreats inside, slamming the door behind him.

Ally's father always treated me good when I was a kid. He knew my father was abusive and even threatened him for beating my mom. I always felt God sent him to protect us. I guess I was wrong, because that all changed when I changed. Ally told me he's the reason she can't hang out with me anymore. Even when Ally and I make friends again, it doesn't appear that I'll be hanging out at her house, and that makes me sad. I was hoping Ally would walk with me to the park, but I'm not waiting around for her after that.

I put my head down and pick up my pace. Sweat has consumed my entire body. It beads from my hairline and runs down my body, in all directions. My shirt is already getting damp and I feel it running down my back, to my bottom. My armpits are soggy and sweat has even beaded on my forearms. As I stare at them, I notice they were a little pink and I wonder if I've gotten a sunburn today. I sigh aloud as the inability to breathe properly makes my discomfort more problematic. I probably should've taken the medicine and gotten the healing process started. Nah, I concede. I would never forgive myself if I'd have gotten sleepy and missed the party. That's going to be a great time and I can't wait to go.

My excitement boils over as I reach the park. My

breathing is heavy and I feel my heart rate is elevated. I know most of it is from the walk over, in this sweltering heat, but the anticipation of rejoining the group is almost too much to bear. I'm so excited.

There's not a single person in the park and I wonder if they're at the fort already. I pull out my phone to check the time and notice that it's five to three. I'm a little early and they're probably running late. Maybe they're nervous too.

I continue forward, toward the picnic table by the big oak tree, hoping it will offer me some shade as I wait for them. The grass is overgrown and I wonder how that's even possible with the heatwave we've been under for the past few weeks. I figure they haven't mowed in quite some time, maybe months. The play area has grass grown through it, and everything looks unkempt. It's been a long time since I've been here. I've only glanced in its direction in passing and never noticed how bad it is. It was such a happy place for me as a kid, with the others, and serves as a reminder that I was left all alone when they shunned me.

The picnic table is well shaded and I pull the water bottle from my back pocket and take a long drink, stopping just short of finishing the entire bottle. My nose runs and I wipe it with my thumb before wiping my thumb across the seat of my shorts to clean it. After taking a seat, the concrete warms my bottom, even though it's shaded, and serves as a reminder of how warm it is outside. Looking across the picnic table, I notice many chips and cracks and wonder when the city will replace it. These old concrete picnic tables must've been hard to deliver.

I place the bag of cookies next to my water bottle and scan the park. After noticing the swings, I can't help but feel nostalgic as I stare at them. Ally and I spent a lot of time on those swings, talking about everything under the sun. We'd sit there for hours and just lightly swing, back and forth, telling stories, and daydreaming about the life we were going to have. We talked about where we'd go and what we planned for college. Even at a young age, we knew we wanted to go together and brave this world with each other to lean on. That's where I told her I was different, and that was the last time I ever spent with her. She didn't take the news very well and her father took it even worse. He said she was never to talk to me again, and that was it. Not another word until earlier this week. The pain of missing her causes tears to well up in my eyes now, as I look forward to spending time with her. I guess it's not just her I want to spend time with, it's all of them. So many memories.

I think of Milo and picture his sweet little face. I feel guilty that I didn't feed him when he asked me to. I pull my phone out of my pocket, open my mom's contact and text her.

"Don't forget to feed Milo when you get home. Give him an extra scoop, please. He looked really hungry. I love you and will text when I know where the party is."

I put my phone back in my pocket and notice an old car has pulled up along the road. They don't get out and I see a man sitting inside, by himself. I wonder how hot he is, sitting in that car. I feel warm, myself, and stand to my feet. After collecting the bag of cookies and the water bottle, I cross the playground. At the opening in the woods, I feel anxious and excited to see everyone. Butterflies churn in my stomach and I can't wait to see them again. This is going to be great.

The path through the woods is narrow and slightly uphill. I hear nothing ahead and figure the group must be running late. Maybe I'll jump out and scare them when they get here. That'll help break the ice. The bag of cookies I carry is making my hand sweat. I switch to the other hand and wipe the sweat across the leg of my shorts. I hold the bag up to inspect the cookies. The heat is melting them and a few have broken into pieces. I really want one and hope the others will be excited to have one too. I know Ally will for sure. They were always her favorite.

The walk up the path, to the fort, isn't far, and just as I crest the top of the hill, I see the fort surrounded by trash and notice that nothing has changed since the last time I was here, which was a long time ago. I feel the nostalgia about the place and can't help but smile as come to a stop and glance around. I finish the bottle of water and toss it to the ground. I'll have to remember to pick it up when I leave. I don't want to add to the trash problem. I have so many happy memories here and it's fitting this will be where we all come back together. I've missed this place. It's tied to my loving memories of our group, and it makes me sad to think about what they did to me. At least they're going to make it right and we can all move on.

All at once, I feel something strike my head and I am thrust forward. Surprised, I'm unable to get my hands out in front of me as my body crashes to the ground and my head bounces off a rock. I reach out for the cookies but can't find them. I hear ringing in my ears as I roll to my back. My vision is blurry, and my eyes flutter before darkness overtakes me.

I feel something warm as it slides over my face and I come to life when it brushes against the wound on my head. I grimace as I groggily reach my hand upward to assess the damage. It's darker under here, but I can clearly see designs on the cloth and smell the fabric softener. As my hand reaches the covering, I feel a hand grab ahold of mine and roll me to my stomach while forcing one arm, and then the other, behind my back.

"What's going on?" I ask, clearly confused and feeling dazed.

I can't think as a knee pins my arms behind me and I barely resist. Before I know it, I hear the familiar sound of duct tape as it's wrapped around and around my wrists, as they're securely fastened behind my back. Unable to comprehend, I don't fight back until it's too late, and my arms are uncomfortably bound behind me. I hear whispers of someone grumbling.

"What are you doing? Help me up."

A sharp jerk sent my head upward, and I felt a pop in my neck. I hear the duct tape as it unravels and my head is shifted to the side.

"Hey! Stop it!" I call out in a fit of panic. "Help! Someone, help me!"

A hand covers my mouth, and a finger hangs between my teeth. Without thought, I bite down and hear a deep voice yell out in pain. Brock, I think, but I can't be sure. Something strikes hard against the back of my head, recoiling my face into the ground, just above my eye socket. I immediately feel the sting, and then the sensation of blood as it seeps from my eyebrow. The impact sent dust into my face covering, and I could clearly smell it. After already being disoriented from the blow to the head, my thoughts are all around me as the sheer pain causes me to cry out in agony.

Again, my head is jerked upward and I hear the duct tape as it starts at my chin and wraps around my mouth. "What are you doing?" I scream out in panic as they wrap it around and around until it securely covers my mouth. The fabric presses firmly against my lips, and as I open my mouth to scream again, they cinch the duct tape across my mouth, directly between my teeth, pulling it tightly against my tongue. I bite as I yell. Fear now replaces my confusion. I wiggle uncontrollably as I attempt to lift my hands to my face, only to fail, as they are bound tightly behind me.

Although I bite at the tape, it's getting tougher to move my jaw as they are continuing to wrap it repeatedly. The cloth has securely meshed against my ears, with multiple layers of tape covering it. I'm unable to hear anything other than murmurs. For another moment, I can still see the light-colored fabric until the tape is bound over my eyes and darkness overtakes me. I can't breathe.

After another pass at eye level, the tape is circled around my head and back to my mouth. I mumble and half scream a muffled cry until the tape finally extinguishes my noise. My head falls to the ground, once again landing firmly on the spot just above my eye. The pain is excruciating, and I cry out in silence. What is going on, I wonder?

Quiet falls and I wiggle in the hot dirt as my sweaty body pulls at the bindings. Fear consumes my thoughts, and I'm unable to focus on anything. I feel my shirt has rolled up, and as I lay face down, my stomach brushes against the rock and grit of the earth beneath me. I focus on the pain of the scrapes and scratches that I envision on my belly. My head pounds and I find it difficult to breathe. I snort through my nose and find solace that somehow the stuffiness has relented and I'm able to take in a small amount of air. While it's barely enough to sustain me, I can finally breathe through my nose. How is that possible, I wonder? I haven't been able to breathe through my nose all day and now I can. At least a little bit.

The kick catches me off guard. The blow glances off of my arm and lands squarely on my side. I hear a scream from someone as I silently cry out in agony. The pain is unbearable, and I fear I've broken a rib; my arm also hurts. Tears well in my eyes, but they're immediately dried by the fabric that is taped securely to my face. I'm hyperventilating. I can barely breathe and find it difficult to draw in a sufficient amount of air, especially now, with my rib hurting. I sob uncontrollably.

I feel hands, first on my left side, rolling me to my side, then on my right as they grip tightly on my arms. I tense and prepare for another attack as they lift me to my knees. I'm begging with them. Pleading them not to hurt me, even though I know they don't understand my words.

Tears are pouring from my eyes as I fear the worst. The screaming voice quiets as they position me upright. My knees are hurting from the rocks underneath, and I worry I'm going to collapse. I feel the dampness in my crotch before it streams down my legs. Although I'm frightened, I still feel the sting of embarrassment, as I know I've pissed myself. I gasp at air through my nostrils while I fight against my sniveling. I feel I must stop crying if I have a chance of catching my breath.

The blow to my stomach catches me off guard. Air and snot fly from my nose and I almost choke, as it has nowhere to escape. The pain is excruciating and as I double over, I'm gripped at my arms and flung backward. I cry out and beg, but hear nothing more. I can't breathe. The blockage completely shuts my mouth's airway, forcing me to draw small amounts of air through my nose. I hyperventilate and call out in horror. How can they do this to me?

The silence is deafening as I lay, not only bound by the tape, but bound with my legs tucked under me. I know I need to roll to my side to get my legs from under my body, but I can't. I have no strength to move. My fear runs rampant as I wait for them to let me loose. Feeling the snot discharge from my nose, I snort hard and expel as much as I can, hoping to increase some type of airflow. The heat is overwhelming and my body aches. My contorted body and tense muscles pull every fiber as I struggle to free myself. My head hurts. I've experienced headaches from some of the medication that doctors had me on, but nothing compares to this. The spot over my eye aches and I feel my heart beating through it. I feel knots on the back of my head and they pound along with my heartbeat, just as though they are in rhythm. My ribs ache and my stomach hurts from not only the punch, but the horror of it all. I feel that I'm going to be sick and attempt to swallow.

I cry out after feeling the release of my bowels. How can this happen to me? I'm so embarrassed and I don't want to sit in it. It makes me sick to my stomach. The thought of it, and the fear of them discovering what I've done. I can't take it. I will never hear the end of this.

I wiggle my hands, hoping to free them. I feel sweat pouring from my arms and pray it loosens the tape. I try to pull, but find it impossible to maneuver them free. My heart races as I suck at air through my nose. Surely, they're going to let me loose. Any minute now. I try to turn on my side, but find it difficult to move an inch. Tears once again pour from my eyes and I sob. What a horrible thing to do to someone. How can they do this to me? We were such good friends, and they did this for what? Because I choose to be me!

I hear a loud groan as I'm hit in the head. The pain is unbearable and I brace myself for another. My mind races, but I can't catch a thought. I need to run. I need to stand to my feet and run. I can't. I'm broken and hurting from all over. Please God. Please help me.

I hear voices, muffled by my hooded binding. Some are higher than others, but I can't make out the words. Feet brush against my body and I roll to my side, attempting to guard myself from another blow. I cry out as fear consumes me. It sounds like only a whisper with the tape gagging my ability to speak. Why would they do this to me?

The gunshot is deafening and my body tenses, from the hair on my head, all the way to my toes. Something is on top of me and the weight of it is heavy. I feel it moved off and don't understand. Where did they shoot me? I wonder? My body aches all over and I can't put my finger on it. Maybe my stomach, as the pain intensifies.

My body trembles as I wait to die. Anxiety pours from my soul. Feeling that I need to calm myself to reduce the panic, I focus on my breathing. Barely able to retrieve any air through my nose, I feel my breath beginning to leave me. The sweat, the piss and shit, the pain and agony that I feel. Not only did they abuse me, they humiliated me, and we were supposed to be friends. Stress creeps over my thoughts and I feel the bile accumulate in the pit of my stomach.

I hear the loud explosion of two more gunshots. My mind falls blank and I hear nothing. Where is Ally? She will save me.

I'm so hot. I need a drink of water, and they need to get this off of my mouth. I can't breathe. The sheer terror I feel is causing me to gasp at the air. I'm going to puke. My mind races in a million directions before finally slowing down. I see us. I see us as kids and playing with one another. I sob uncontrollably as I think of them. I won't say anything if they'll let me go. I just want to live and I want to go home.

I feel lightheaded and a sense of ease washes over me as I think of home. My breathing has shortened and I feel the vomit climbing, climbing up my throat. I see my mom and my grandma with their loving faces. And there is Milo. I smile as I imagine him standing over me, licking at my face. I want to go home. I want to see my best friend and hold him tightly.

Dear God, I worry. Who will look after Milo? I'm going to miss him so much.

Millie Connor

"Millie, get up!"

The sound of my mother's voice stabs into my dream, like a hundred nails to my ears. I pull the blanket over my head. "I'm sleeping. Leave me alone!"

"You get out of bed right now. It's afternoon."

I'm surprised to hear the time, but I still don't want to wake up. I'm so sleepy and I was having such a glorious dream.

"Millie, I'm not kidding!" she yells as she jerks the blanket from my body.

I cover my eyes as the sunlight overwhelms my senses and I wiggle around. I reach to my feet and grab the blanket before flopping backward on the bed and covering my face once again. "Leave me alone!"

For the second time, she jerks the blanket from over me. Coming to life, I sit up and glare at her. "Fine!" I jump out of bed and march across the room, gripping at my door knob and pointing to the hallway. "Get out!"

She shakes her head and begins making my bed. While she fluffs my pillows, she stares back at me. "Where were you last night?"

I grit my teeth and glare at her. Angrily, I step into the hallway and slam the door shut behind me, with her on the other side. I quickly march down the hall and duck into the bathroom. I close the door behind me and twist the lock. My head hurts and I feel a little queasy. I step to the toilet and pull down my pajama shorts. The toilet seat is cold and as I pee, I hear a knock on the door.

"Millie," she calls out. "You better change your attitude."

I inhale deeply through my nose. "I'm going to the restroom. Leave me alone!"

I hear her footsteps trail off as she disappears down the hallway. After swirling my tongue around my mouth, I wince at the terrible taste it produces. I drank too much last night and my mouth tastes horrible. When I finish, I pull up my shorts and glimpse into the toilet before flushing. It's bright orange and I worry that I've dehydrated myself. I've been drinking booze all week, with barely any water, and it's been so hot outside. I may need to get some Pedialyte to make me feel better. I have a party tonight and it's going to be a good one. Caden's parties are always epic.

I wash my hands as I stare at my reflection in the mirror. My eyeshadow is smeared and I look as if I have two black eyes. I lean over and splash water on my face, taking time to wipe at my eyeshadow, hoping it comes off. Seeing barely any improvement, I pull a makeup remover wipe from the counter and go to work. Still tasting the badness of my mouth, I make a sour face. As I watch my reflection in the mirror, it makes me giggle at the sight of myself. I'm a hot mess and ready for more.

After drying my face, I wet my toothbrush and

begin brushing my teeth. The events of last night replay in my mind. All the boys wanted me, I think. Especially when I danced on the diving board and was the center of attention. I smile as I remember them drooling over me. I seduced each of them with just a few movements of my hips. Even the ones with girlfriends. I saw Caden looking, even after Ally covered his eyes. We shouldn't have anything but pool parties this time of year, especially with the heat we've had lately. And, I like any opportunity I get to show my body off.

I rinse my toothbrush and step to the door. I inhale deeply, holding the air in my lungs for longer than I should as I exit and make my way to the kitchen. I'm hungry. I don't think I ate anything yesterday other than that bag of hot Cheetos.

"Where were you last night?" my mom repeats herself as I enter the kitchen and make a beeline for the refrigerator.

I sigh aloud, not wanting to get into it with her this morning. "I was with Ally," I answer. "I told you I was going with her."

She doesn't let up. "Where?" she questions.

"We were at Madison's, gosh!" I exclaim. "We swam and watched a movie."

I pull a bottle of orange juice from the refrigerator and walk next to her as she gazes at me. Reaching over her head, I pull a glass out of the cabinet and leave the door open. She can shut it if she wants. I don't want to stand next to her.

"Madison's parents were out of town last night," she continues. "I don't think they would've liked you being over there when they're not home."

I roll my eyes and don't feel the need to respond as I fill the cup with juice. I place the container on the counter next to the lid and take a long drink. It tastes good and further advances my concern that I'm dehydrated.

"We were worried sick about you. What time did you get home?"

I take another drink and glance at her sideways. She really will not let this go. If I wasn't so hungover and able to think, I wouldn't have told her where the party was. I should've said I was at Brooke's and we wouldn't be having this conversation right now. I pull the glass from my mouth and lick my lips. "Maybe midnight," I lie.

"No, you didn't," she quickly responds, calling me on my bluff. "Your father and I were up until one, waiting on you when you wouldn't answer your phone." She slams the cabinet door. "You came home at three in the morning and I heard you stumble down the hallway."

I glance over at her before turning back to the refrigerator.

"You can't be out drinking all hours of the night and driving around. You'll kill someone."

I slam the refrigerator door closed. "I wasn't driving!" I yell. "Caden and Ally brought me home."

She crosses her arms as she leans against the counter. "Was he drinking?"

I calm myself as I lie to her again. "No. Ally called him to come and get us. He was playing video games at home."

My mother exhales and glares at me. I think I see her soften as she moves down the counter and puts the lid on the orange juice before returning it to the refrigerator. "Just be careful," she says. "You have your whole life ahead of you."

I smile in knowing that she's weakening. I'll be off to college soon, and then I won't have to worry about her interfering. "I will. I promise."

Our conversation falls as she stares at me blankly. I'm happy to hear her phone ring in the other room and smirk as she walks out of the room to get it. She won't be back, I hope. That should be my dad calling her to meet him for lunch. As cheesy as it is, they meet every single day for a late lunch. I'll never let my husband dictate when I get to eat. That's if I even get married. I don't know why anyone would want to be tied down to one person for the rest of their life.

I return to the refrigerator and open the freezer. I'm starving and hope to find something to eat. I notice my mom went grocery shopping, and it's packed full. After moving things around, I scrunch my nose as I struggle to find something that sounds appetizing. It's nothing but frozen, processed garbage. I'm not putting that in my body.

After closing the freezer door, I open the refrigerator and scan the shelves. Located directly behind the orange juice, I find a single serving dinner salad. That'll work, I think. I'm on a mission to lose a couple of pounds before we return to school. I'm already there, but I don't want to lose any ground. I want to look as good as I can at the start of my senior year.

Removing the plastic from the top is not a simple task. I just got new nails yesterday, and I can't grip the tab. I slide over a few steps and remove a fork from the silverware drawer. I stab into the top and it punctures the plastic easily. Maybe a little too easy since the ranch packet is damaged after I remove the top. Oh well, I would not use it anyway, since I have fat-free dressing in the refrigerator. Some people say it's not good for you, but I don't care as long as I don't get fat.

Once I've removed the ham and cheese packets, I toss them on the counter before I sprinkle the carrots across the lettuce. I shuffle over to the refrigerator and pull my salad dressing from the door. It doesn't taste very good, but I can make it work. After drizzling the top, I lay the bottle down and stir my salad before returning to the table. Just as

I pick up my phone, my mother reappears in the doorway with her purse slung over her shoulder.

"I'm going to meet your dad for lunch," she calls out. "We'll wait on you if you want to get dressed."

I shake my head, but don't answer. I return my eyes to my phone and open Instagram.

I hear my mom sigh and glance up to see her enter the kitchen. She collects the trash that I left on the counter and puts it in the can. "Don't leave a mess in here, and I'll see you when I get back."

I nod in agreement as I watch her return the bottle of salad dressing to the refrigerator. I can't help but smile as I watch her waddle out of the kitchen. I won't be here when she gets home. I'm going to the gym as soon as I finish this salad and the party tonight is going to be epic. Caden is throwing a bash at his grandpa's cabin, down by the creek. There's a sizeable area for swimming, and he's been down there for two days, stacking up wood for a bonfire. It's going to be a blast.

As I scroll through Instagram, I fight the urge to post a snapshot of my salad. I don't look beautiful at the moment and I don't think I'll get many likes from a picture of lettuce. I stop scrolling on a post from a woman I follow. She's always so trendy. She eats at the nicest restaurants, wears the nicest clothes, and posts pictures with a bunch of different men. She lives in Chicago and is self-sufficient, just like I aspire to be. She's never been married and looks like she has the best time ever. It's weird because she's a middle-aged woman about the same age as my mom. They couldn't be more different, though. She's sophisticated and trendy, where my mom is, well, my mom.

I feel bad for my mom. She's only in her early forties and she doesn't work. She takes care of the house and looks after me, since I'm their only child. She's stuck up my butt and won't back off. I guess I'm all she has. She's not as pretty as me and I wonder where I get my looks from. She's short and chubby, and sometimes I get embarrassed to be seen with her. She's really let herself go. Sure, she dresses nice, but you can tell a lot about a person by how they maintain their body. I don't know what my dad sees in her. He stayed in shape throughout his life and could probably trade her in for a younger one. He loves her, though. I just don't understand why.

After finishing the salad, I put my fork and glass in the sink before tossing the container in the garbage. Don't want to hear mom complain about it if I leave it on the table. I return to the refrigerator and search for a bottle of water. Coming up empty, I see nothing but cheap spring water and close the door. I hope mom didn't forget to get my Smartwater. I'll be pissed if she did. I open the cupboard and happily find a fresh case, sitting just at my feet, on the floor. I can't believe she didn't put it in the refrigerator, but I guess I'll have to drink it. I lean down and rip the package open before retrieving one bottle. My mouth tastes horrible after having orange juice with the non-fat dressing. I'll have to remember not to do that again. The flavor combination is terrible.

I return to the cabinet for a cup. There's a wide selection of tumblers, but I can only find two in the cabinet. I bet they're all in my car or in my room; I think to myself and laugh. I need to bring them in so mom can wash them. I pick out the prettiest of the two and take it to the refrigerator and fill it with ice. After returning to the counter, I pull the lid from the bottle and take a long drink before pouring the rest into the cup. While holding the cup to eye level, I decide I like its color. It's purple with pink flowers. It'll go nice with my purple bikini, so that's what I'll wear to the party tonight. I return the lid on and suck through the straw. The water has already turned cold and is very refreshing. I need to drink plenty of water today.

Choosing not to shower is easy. Since I need to work out, I will just shower at the gym. They have better water pressure, anyway. However, I felt like I needed to brush my teeth again, my mouth still tastes horrible. I step into the bathroom and wet my toothbrush. As I glance in the mirror, I notice my hair is a mess. While holding the toothbrush between my teeth, I grab a hair tie from the sink and slip it over my wrist. Using both hands, I smooth out my hair and pull it tightly behind my head. When I have it securely in place, I fold it over and wrap it with the hair tie.

While I brush, I retreat to my bedroom and remove my sleeping shorts. I step to my dresser and pull out a pair of yoga pants. They're designed for appearance and not necessarily for performance, but I can manage. As I turn, I catch a glimpse of myself in the mirror. Turning to the side, I stick my butt out and give it a slap. God, I have a great ass. I slip my shirt off and replace it with a sports bra that matches my leggings. This will look great in my Instagram picture, I think. I grab my bag and fill it with another pair of leggings and a sports bra to change into at the gym. I want people to know that I've been to the gym. I just don't want to wear my stinky clothes when I finish. While sitting on the bed, I lace up my sneakers as I continue brushing. The bed feels comfortable and I really want to climb on top and go back to sleep. Snapping to it, I grab my bag and my tumbler as I head for the bathroom to rinse my mouth.

After stepping off the porch, I walk to the car and I'm immediately overwhelmed with heat. It's so hot out here and I hate my life. I pick up my pace and jog to my car, hoping to get the air going as quickly as possible. Because my car is parked dangerously close to my father's boat, I run around the back of it to avoid slipping between them. Stepping to the door, I reach for the handle and immediately burn my fingertips. I let go and curse as I wipe my hand against my leg. Not one to give up, I hold my breath as I reach for it again and swing the door open.

The burst of heat that hits me in the face is almost unbearable, but it's nothing compared to when I climb inside. The leather burns my behind as I put my foot on the brake and push start. I toss my bag into the passenger seat and place my cup in the holder before closing the door. The heat is intense as I crank the air to high and roll all four windows down. Hoping to get some air into the car, I quickly put it in gear and back out of the driveway. When I place my hand on the steering wheel, the heat instantly consumes my palm and burns worse than the door handle. Stomping on the brake, I don't know how I'm going to steer it. I reach behind me to the floorboard and feel around before finding some fabric. As I lift it to me, my arm brushes against the console and burns me for a third time. Grasping to the fabric, I bring it to eyesight and chuckle when I recognize it as a pair of my bikini bottoms. Oh well, I think and wrap it around the steering wheel before continuing my back out of the driveway.

The ride to the gym is blistering. I'm sweating everywhere, and I mean everywhere. The air blowing through the window is hot and I can't seem to cool down. The air conditioning hasn't gotten cold yet and I'm nearing heat exhaustion. The temperature inside the car is comparable to a furnace, and I'm miserable. What a horrible way to die, I think. To suffocate may be one of the worst. I find it hard to breathe in here and I have the window down.

Since it's near to home, in only a few minutes, I pull up in front of the gym and cut the engine. Being that it's on the square, and the police station is nearby, I leave the window down. I don't want a repeat of heat, like I did on the drive over here. Especially after I finish my workout and freshly showered.

Once I've dropped my bag off in the locker room, I find a yoga mat and roll it out for some light stretching.

When I'm satisfied that I've limbered my body, I position my phone to record myself as I exaggerate my stretches for the camera. I work diligently to appear sensual as I slowly contort my body to angles that it shouldn't bend, always keeping my butt in the video, since it's my best feature. Satisfied that I have what I need, I drop to my backside and pick up my phone. Following a short round of editing, I post the video to my story. #stretched

Now that I'm loose, I get to the real workout. I don't half ass it at the gym. Most people see me as this skinny little girl, but I'm serious about my physique. I plan to move away for college and if I want to rise in the social ranks, I'm going to need to be a cheerleader at a major university. Still to this day, I take gymnastics and hope to improve my form as I head into my senior year of high school. Although my parents aren't poor, we don't have a lot of money and I hope to get a scholarship by being the best. With football starting soon, I need to get lots of video of myself performing the best routines so I can send it out to schools. I don't want to miss a single opportunity, and after Caden's party tonight, I'm going to cool it on the drinking. I'll still hang out, but I need to cut back.

Once I've finished a solid workout and have a good deal of sweat, I move back to the squat machine and reduce the weight on the bar. I start the camera and position my phone behind me to once again capture my best feature. When I think I have enough footage to make a good video, I collect my phone and rewatch what I've captured. At about halfway through, I notice a guy bends over, next to my workout, to get one of the weights. He realized he was in my video and quickly exited, but the content was ruined.

"Stupid bitch," I mutter to myself before deleting the video and setting it up to rerecord. I hope they'll stay out of my shot on this one.

Satisfied with the next video, I edit on my way to the

locker room. I take a seat on the bench as I add a few finishing touches and post the video to my feed. #squats #dumptruck

With Instagram taken care of, I strip off and wrap myself with a towel. I take a long drink from my cup and set it on the bench before heading down the hallway to the tanning bed. This place is nice, but the one thing I think they can do better is make the tanning beds for women only. I don't like tan lines and I strip down to naked while I tan. I've had a man walk in on me before. Honestly, it didn't bother me that much, but he was beside himself. Although, I'm sure he liked what he saw. I don't know why a man would want to tan, but whatever. They need their own area and leave ours alone. I find it gross to have to tan where a sweaty man does.

As I lay on the bed and pull the door closed over the top of me, a sense of peace washes over and I'm happy. I'm always going, going, going and I never take a minute for myself. I don't have a job, but it takes a lot of work for me to look this good. I have gymnastics; I work out, and I'm social in everything that I do. I take a long time to get myself ready and I don't know how I'm going to make everything work in college.

I plan to attend college out in California, and I won't take no for an answer. If I have to, I'll rack up a crazy amount of student loans and daddy will just have to pay what he can. I know he and mom will miss me, but I just can't take this town. I'm way too big for it and destined to do great things. I would like to stay single, but I'm not opposed to marrying a college athlete that might make the pros. At least for a little while, anyway. I think I'll get a business degree and go into real estate. You can make a lot of money in real estate, especially if you're pretty like me. I want to travel the world and see as much as I can in this short life. I need money to do that.

I like Caden but he's taken by Ally. If anyone has a chance around here to make it to the pros, it's him. Although I like the way he looks at me, I could never do that to Ally. She's one of my best friends and I'd never forgive myself. I am going to have to cool it when I'm drunk though. I like to flirt, and I don't know if I could push him away if he approached me.

The only other boy in this hillbilly infested town that might make it is Brock. I doubt it, but he is really good at football. I love Brock, but not like that. That would be gross since he's been my friend since forever and feels more like a brother. He is good looking, but he has such a horrible personality. I think he's angry with life. Especially after his father left, and they went from poor to poorer. There's seriously something off with him, but I love him.

After nearly falling asleep in the tanning bed, I return to the locker room and drop my towel at the door of the shower. I'll get a new one when I get out and that one will help me dry my feet when I finish. I turn the water on and adjust the temperature. After stepping underneath the spray, I find a used bottle of shampoo on the shelf. It's a good one and an expensive brand. I never bring my own soap or shampoo. I always use whatever the other people have in here. When I finish washing my hair, I lather up and wash my body as I look forward to this evening. It's going to be so much fun and I've had my eye on a farm boy that just moved to town not long ago. He doesn't have any money and his parents work for the O'Malley's, but he'll do for tonight, anyway.

Feeling content that I'm thoroughly clean, I cut the water and step out of the shower. I wipe my feet on the towel at the base of the door and continue across the floor, leaving droplets of water behind me as I go. After I towel off, I step in front of the mirror and begin blow drying my hair. At five foot eight, I'm taller than most girls in the school. I'm slim but toned and always have a good tan, thanks to this gym. My hair is darker and I have a lot of it. Not only is the hair on my head thick, so are my eyebrows and my arm hair is dark, which prompts me to shave my arms as frequently as I shave my legs. If not tended to regularly, my hair can overtake me and make me appear as homely as my mother. I don't know why I was blessed with such healthy hair, but I feel that it's actually a curse.

As I retreat to the bench for my clothes and makeup bag, an older woman sits close to my belongings. While still naked, I step next to her and notice she flashes a dirty look in my direction as she slides along the bench, away from me. Not one for taking shit from anyone. I glare at her.

"What?" I ask. "Do you have a problem?"

She scrunches her nose and shakes her head as she rises from the bench and walks out of the locker room without saying a single word.

"That's what I thought, bitch."

While rifling through my bag, I notice I didn't bring any underwear. Oh well, I think. It'll be cooler without them and I won't have to worry about panty lines showing through my leggings. I dress quickly and take my make-up bag with me to the mirror. I first brush my hair and, once again, pull it tightly behind me in a ponytail. Afterward, I apply my make-up and I'm able to work quickly. One of the first Instagram reels I started was a make-up tutorial, so I used to make a video, clean it off, and repeat the process four or five times. At this point, I'm a pro and know exactly how to accentuate the curves of my face. After applying the finishing touches, I can't help but be impressed at how good I've become. I look hot and I've transformed myself from slightly above average to definitely a ten. I blow myself a kiss in the mirror and turn on my heels before grabbing my bag and exiting the gym.

As I step out onto the sidewalk, I feel lightheaded,

and the sheer temperature appears to melt my skin. I sure hope it doesn't cause my make-up to run. I hurry to the car and toss my bag inside before turning toward the pharmacy. It's only a couple of buildings away from the gym, so I jog, hoping to find their air conditioning quickly. As I reach for the door, it opens and I leap to the side to keep from getting hit by the door. It's our new police chief. I think her name is Kelley.

"Sorry about that," she apologizes as she holds the door for me. "I didn't see you there."

"No worries," I respond with a giant smile. "I'm quick as a cat!"

She simply nods and takes off walking. I figure to see her cross the street toward the courthouse, but she doesn't. She climbs in her cruiser and pulls away. What a bitch, I think before entering the store. She didn't even give me a courtesy laugh.

After only being in the heat for a few minutes, the air inside feels amazing and I tilt my head back, soaking it up as a fan overhead blows right in my face.

"Hey girl!"

I turn toward the voice and recognize Amber. I forgot she worked here. I think her parents own the pharmacy, but I'm not sure. "Hey," I answer back. "It's so hot outside."

She drops her phone to the counter and nods her head in agreement. "Too hot," she says. "It'll be nice to get down to the creek tonight. Are you going?"

I give her a blank look. "Of course. It's not a party without me."

She smiles and speaks, but I don't want to hear any more small talk, so I cut her off. "I need some Pedialyte. Do you have any?"

"Yeah," she nods and points toward the back. "It's on the back wall by the diapers."

I glance to where she points and really don't want to walk to get it. I turn back to her. "Can you grab me a bottle?"

"Sure," she answers as she slides from behind the counter and moves quickly toward the back of the room. "What flavor do you want?"

"What do you have?" I ask while speaking loud enough for her to hear.

"Um, let me check."

I watch her walk down the aisle and stare at her backside. She is a pretty little thing and I see the boys watching her too. She's a couple of years younger than me and she's a cheerleader as well. I find her as my biggest competition in school, outside of Ally. Ally is by far the most beautiful, but she already has Caden. I swear those two will get married and have kids right out of high school. What a waste.

"We have grape, berry, and fruit punch," she calls out.

"Ooh, fruit punch," I reply, and it makes me happy that they have my favorite.

She smiles as she makes her way back to the counter, and I can't help but snicker at how far she'll go for me. Although I don't care much for her, she looks up to me as the cheer captain and will do anything I ask. It's ridiculous and I have no respect for her. I never kissed anyone's butt when I was coming up. She shouldn't either.

"You just missed the freak," she announces as she returns to the counter.

Not understanding, I can't help but ask. "Huh?"

"The freak," she repeats through a wide grin. "You know, Sammy."

"Oh," I nod, now understanding what she means. I unlock my phone to pull up my debit card.

She sees me open my phone and speaks up. "The

tap to pay is down. We can only take cash or cards."

Although my wallet is just outside, in my car, I shake my head. "I only have this."

"That's OK," she returns. "You can just pay me later."

I tilt my head and take a step back as I put on a big smile. "Awe. You're so sweet. Thank you." I turn to exit.

"I asked him if he wanted any tampons?"

I turn back to face her and see her laughing. "You did what?"

"I asked him if he wanted any tampons or testosterone," she laughs. "Right in front of the chief."

I fake a smile and roll my eyes. "That's not very polite," I respond. "That's not very Christian of you."

The smile quickly fades from her face as I turn and walk out of the door, hearing that stupid bell as leave. I smile in knowing I made her feel bad.

The oven like heat inside the car is overwhelming, even after leaving the window down. As I back out of the parking spot, I see Amber peering through the window. She's staring at me as if I kicked her dog. I smile and wave as I put the car in gear and speed down the street.

The air is scorching as it blows on my face and I feel sweat escaping my body. Leggings were not a good idea and not having underwear on has given zero relief. If anything, it makes me more uncomfortable as the red-hot seat makes my butt crack sweat and there's nothing to soak it up. My house is just a few blocks down the road and I pass it by as I spot Sam leaning against a fence outside of the daycare. I slow the car as I peer in his direction. My god, I think. He's gotten fat and looks really uncomfortable.

I quickly press on the gas and speed away, turning the corner to circle back to my house and hoping not to be seen. I feel bad for him. He's had it rough since he transitioned and things haven't been the same. I don't know why anyone would want to do that to themselves when they live in a small town like this, but I also don't know why it's such a big deal to any of these hillbillies. People should be able to live how they want. Life is short, and a person deserves to be happy.

If I were Sam, I wouldn't have told anyone until I moved away, but that's just me. I wouldn't want anyone judging me like that. He just made himself a target, and believe me, these people like taking their shortcomings out on others.

I kind of knew, though. It wasn't that big of a surprise when he came out. I always knew he was different. I don't really care what Sam wants to do with his life. I just can't let him bring me down in the process. I have too much at stake.

I miss him, and sometimes I think about him, and hope he's doing OK. We had such a great time together when we were kids and it was the six of us. There's something nice about having that many close friends. It's comforting, and it's empowering. There's strength in numbers. Although, I guess we didn't miss him too much when we cut him out of the group. We were all pretty sad at first, but we got over it and there's not a lot of difference between five and six. The five of us have been close ever since and we'll probably remain friends for the rest of our lives. We're pretty good at accepting each other for what we are. Well, I guess we're not that good. Look at what we did to Sam.

I dread meeting with him this afternoon. It's going to be so awkward and I don't like awkward. Ally says we need to get together before we all go away to college, but I don't know about it. I think we should just leave it alone. Sam seems to be doing just fine, and I don't really want judgement from people outside of the group for being friends with him.

The air is beginning to blow cold as I near my driveway. I still have a couple of hours before we meet. I was going to run around all day, but I think I'll just hang out on the couch and scroll through Instagram while I wait. I sure hope mom has other things to do and leaves me alone. I don't feel like going anywhere else and I don't want to be out in this heat any more than I need to. I'll leave if she bothers me, but I hate the idea of being out in this heat. I think I'll drink this entire bottle of Pedialyte so that I'm in prime shape for the party tonight. It's going to be so much fun.

Brooke Riley

After stepping out of the shower, I quickly dry my body before wrapping a towel around my head and another around my body. While poking my head out the door, I glance both ways down the hallway before darting across to my bedroom. I close the door behind me and twist the lock.

As I pull the towel from my head, I dry my hair as much as possible before tossing it in the hamper. I scamper to my dresser and pull out a pair of underwear and a bra. They aren't matching, but it won't matter since no one will see them, anyway. I remove the towel from my body and step through my underwear, pulling them as high as they'll go. I still feel damp and think to myself that I should've dried off better. As I cinch the bra around me, I step in front of the mirror and put the straps over my shoulder. I reach for a brush on the vanity and begin brushing at my hair. While it's still wet, my hair forms to my skull and runs straight down my back. After glancing at the brush, I notice it's full of long strands of my hair and step forward to the mirror as I inspect my scalp. At seventeen, I can't believe how much my hair is thinning and cannot wait to get the collagen that my mother ordered for me. I smooth out the sides and poke it behind my ear. At least my hair isn't bushy, I think. Usually redheads like me have full, kinky hair, but mine is silky smooth. I just don't want to lose any more of it.

I squirt a few blobs of lotion on my hand and lather them up. Starting at my legs, I rub in the lotion all the way up my body. As I cross my stomach, I feel the softness of my belly and fear that I'm gaining too much weight. I've been working at my father's trucking company all summer and haven't gone to the gym a single time. I should go with Millie, since she goes every day, but I can't count on her to be on time. She sleeps most of the day and keeps her own schedule. That would drive me crazy and I think I'll just ask her to give me some exercises to get started.

I nod in agreeing with the plan I set for myself to get more exercise. A person can't be short and fat at the same time, it just doesn't look good. And since there's nothing I can do about my height, I'll have to focus on the weight. Reaching back to my vanity, I grab my clothes from the back of the chair that I laid out last night. It's just a simple dress suit and I dread wearing it today. Although I like to dress nice, I noticed on the weather app this morning that it's supposed to be the hottest day on record, and I dread the heat this suit will generate. This material is not very forgiving and I don't want to sit in sweat all day. Oh well, I think. I'll try to stay inside with the air conditioning until I get home. I must look professional for my father's business. I pray we get some relief from it soon, though. It's been so hot the past few weeks that I just can't stand it anymore.

I hear a knock at my door before my father's voice

sounds out. "Brooky," he calls. "Your mom said breakfast will be ready in five minutes."

"OK," I return. "I'll be right there."

After getting dressed quickly, I delay blow drying my hair until after breakfast. I'm starving this morning and I suppose it won't hurt anything to start my diet at lunchtime.

Stepping into the kitchen, I notice that I'm the last to arrive. My father sits and works on his phone, while my three brothers fidget at the table. My mother is finishing up at the stove and I take a seat next to my youngest brother, Jacob. He's six and immediately reaches out to hug me. While embracing him back, I glance across the table at my twin brothers to see they're both scribbling on a single sheet of paper. They're each ten years old and mirror images of one another. Although people struggle to tell them apart, I notice many differences between the two and have no trouble whatsoever. I chuckle as I watch them draw as a team and work in unison. I wonder if their brains just work that way. Do they really know how the other one feels and what he thinks?

Already on the table in front of me, I spot a heaping pile of bacon and it smells delicious. Turning in my chair, I watch my mother walk toward us with a mountain of pancakes, and I regret sleeping in and not helping her. I know it's only seven in the morning, but we rise early in this house. We each have a roll and we work together to make it happen.

Without a word spoken, my mother glances at my father, who looks up from his phone. We lock hands and bow our heads. As my father speaks, I feel Jacob turn loose and I open one eye to spy on him. He's after a piece of bacon and stares at me with a mischievous grin. I reach out and take the bacon from his fingertips and return his hand to my side, gripping tightly and nodding for him to close his eyes.

I bow my head and hear my father speak, but don't listen to his words. As he mumbles a blessing over our breakfast and our family, I speak my own prayer. With the thought of meeting Sam weighing heavily on my heart, it's her I pray for. I pray that she'll see the faults in her ways and be delivered from evil.

"Thank you, honey," my mother states once my father finishes. "Let's eat."

I help Jacob get a few strips of bacon and place a pancake on his plate. While he grips tightly at the syrup bottle, I allow him to pour it while keeping my hand near the bottom, hoping to guide it on his pancake and not across the table. When I think he's had enough, I take the bottle from his hand and watch as he digs in with the enthusiasm of a six-year-old.

Still grinning at the sight of him, I fill his juice cup from the pitcher before filling mine and offering it to my father. He declines and I notice he's still drinking coffee. He likes it black with no sugar or creamer, and I do not know how he can stomach it.

Feeling famished, yet still hoping to begin my diet, I pull two strips of bacon for myself and the smallest pancake I can find. I smile and feel good for at least making a better choice and hope to improve from it. After drizzling the syrup over the top of the pancake, I add a bit over the top of the bacon. Just as my little brother does, I like syrup.

"Brooky," my father calls out. "I won't be in until noon today. I have to run to the city and deliver a check. We're buying two new trucks today."

He's smiling and I can see that he's pleased with another opportunity to grow his business. I'm very proud of him.

"I won't be in until one or so, myself," my mother adds. "I have a delivery at the boutique and need to meet the driver. It'll take a little longer than usual because I'd like to show the new girl how to stock the inventory and I don't trust that Susan will show her properly."

I nod as my father continues. "I'll bring lunch when I get back."

I smile because hearing it makes me happy. We usually make our lunch and take it with us to save money. I like to eat food from restaurants and rarely get the opportunity. I mean, how many times can a person eat tuna salad before they grow to hate it? "Just a salad, please. I'm going on a diet."

My father scoffs in return. "A salad. Nobody needs to eat that rabbit food for a meal. Are you sure you don't want something else?"

"Just the salad," I answer and can't help but think that he should only have a salad too. Both he and my mom are bigger people and I worry they won't be around for my children to get to know them. They eat unhealthily and they're constantly stressed with the four businesses we own. That's not good for anyone.

"OK, darlin'," he agrees. "A salad it is." He grins and glances toward the end of the table and questions my mother. "Do you want a salad, too?"

She shakes her head and grins in return. "Don't worry about me. I'll figure something out."

My father nods and begins working on his pancakes. He takes a little longer than the rest of us, since he likes peanut butter spread over the top, and plenty of it. As he lathers them with a thick layer, he talks with my twin brothers. They're starting baseball soon and he used to be a pretty good ballplayer, according to him and all the folks around town. I sure hope he slows down a little and works with the boys more. Not only will it make them better, but they'll enjoy spending the time with him.

"Brooke," my mother calls out, catching my attention. "You know what to do when we're not there, right?"

I nod. "Yes, ma'am."

"Good," she smiles. "You listen to whatever Chad has to say and if you have a question, you call me or dad."

"Yes ma'am," I repeat and smile at the fact that she told me what to do, anyway.

I know my job at the trucking company and I'm pretty good at it. I think I can take on more responsibility, but I'm starting school soon. I don't want them to rely on me since they're going to have to hire someone to fill my role now.

"Oh, I almost forgot," I add. "I'm leaving at two today. Me and the guys are going swimming at Caden's grandpa's cabin, and I'm staying the night at Ally's."

My mother nods as my father speaks up. "Look how it all worked out," he says. "Me and your mom will be back in plenty of time to get you out of there early." He stares down his nose at me. "Does Mr. Astor know that ya'll are swimming out there?"

I shrug my shoulders, not wanting to lie to them any more than I have to. I can't tell them it's a party and I certainly can't tell them I'm going to meet Sam. They wouldn't like that at all. We're Christians and cannot abide by that sin.

"I don't know," I admit. "Caden and his grandpa are pretty close, so I'm sure he told him." I didn't lie about that. Caden is close to his grandpa, and I doubt that he'd care if he throws a party. They'd let him get away with murder.

"OK then," he replies. "I'm sure you're right." His smile returns and he bites off a piece of bacon. "Mr. Astor is a good old man," he states. "The whole family is good. Good as gold."

I smile and nod in agreement. He's not wrong. Caden's entire family has been around for my entire life. Somehow, we're always intertwined. Our families do a little business together and Caden and I have gone to school with each other since kindergarten and we've always kept our little group of friends. We're tight and lean on one another. Always have and I hope we always will. Of course, I'd like to see him walk a little closer to the Lord but I think Ally can get him there.

"One more thing," my mom speaks. "Can you drop your brothers off at daycare? I need to run by the bank first thing and pick up new checks for the salon. Sheila has been out, and I need to get it done."

I agree, and we continue to eat our breakfast. We keep constant conversation and laugh together at a story that my father tells. It's about an accident that one driver got into. Thankfully, no one was hurt, but the events surrounding the accident are quite funny, and my father tells a great story. I think that's why he's been so successful in his life. He's a hard worker, but he's also a great salesman.

After we've finished, I help my mother clear the table and rinse the dishes off before putting them in the dishwasher. My father directs my brothers to take out the trash and helps them tidy the house as my mother and I get the kitchen cleaned up. We talk about school and work, before the conversation turns to grandma.

"Do you want to go with me to see grandma this Saturday?" she asks.

"I would, I miss grandma," I admit. I miss her and haven't seen her in a while. I want to spend time with her, but I'm always worried about seeing Sam up there. I don't want to talk to her and she's always looking at me with those puppy dog eyes. It breaks my heart, but she has to learn from her mistakes.

My mother rubs me on the back. "Me too," she agrees. "We've all been so busy lately and I feel terrible leaving her up there by herself. It's just not right."

I nod and can't agree more. "I wish she would just

move in here with us."

"Me too," she repeats. "But she won't. Says she doesn't want to be a burden." She bites her lip. "I think she likes hanging out with the other old folks. Gives her something to do and helps her stay in touch with people her own age."

We talk about grandma for another few minutes, until we've finished cleaning, and I say my goodbyes as I climb the stairs to fix my hair. It's going to take me a minute since it's mostly dried and I need to get it right. I must look presentable when I work the front desk. It's important that a person looks nice if they're the first thing a customer sees. Well, it's very few customers, mostly drivers. But I still need to look good for my father.

As I fix my hair, I think about all the things I want to accomplish this school year. It's only my junior year but I want to apply to colleges early to get a jump on things. I've been class president since my freshman year and I don't expect that to change. Next year, when I'm senior class president, I really want to make a difference and leave a legacy that I'd be happy for people to remember me by. I want to change things for the school and leave it in better shape than I found it. I have a few ideas, but none are the game changer that I search for.

I stay pretty busy with school. I'm a member of the national honor society and have never received a grade lower than an A. I carry a 4.0 GPA and I'm a member of almost every club we have in our district. DECA is my favorite and the key club is my least. FFA's not bad, I guess. It's fun, but not something I would do as a profession any longer. I think farming would be a rewarding field, but I want a business degree. I want to come back home and work with my family to grow our businesses and incorporate more growth. I hope to get married and have him move back with me. I love this town, but there's not a boy within fifty miles that I would consider as husband material.

He's going to have to be a God-fearing man and hard-working, like my father. We go to church every opportunity we get. We go twice on Sunday and every Wednesday, only to miss if we can't walk. My husband must have the same devotion. I want to raise a big family, just like my own, and in this tight-knit community, just as I grew up in. This is a great place to live and the people around here are great, too.

When I finish with my hair, I wrangle my brothers into my car and pull out of the driveway. Both my mother and father are already gone, and I don't want to be late. It's a short drive to the daycare and I try to make it as happy for them as I can. I play music we all like and we each sing along. I'm a much better singer than the three of them, but they're still young and might catch up. I like to sing. I sing in the choir at church and in the choir at school. The school choir is fairly small and we don't get to do much, but I get my fill of singing with the church. We practice a few times each week and I think we're pretty good together.

After shuffling my brothers off to daycare, I hammer down with hopes of not being late to work. Of course, I stay at the speed limit, I just accelerate fast to get up to speed. I don't want a speeding ticket on my impeccable record. That wouldn't sit well with me.

Although I'm not the first to arrive, I'm still ahead of when we actually open. Chad greets me at the door and follows me to the coffeepot after I drop my bag by my desk.

"Need you to run back into town," he says as I pour coffee into a Styrofoam cup. "Have a fuel tank at the parts store." He shakes his head. "I don't know how you destroy a fuel tank like that, but he did it. And that truck has to be in California tomorrow morning."

"Where's Jake?" I ask, clearly confused. "He's still our part's guy, isn't he?"

Chad starts laughing and places his hand on his hips. "Ole Jake is locked up right now."

Caught off guard and clearly surprised, I can't help but ask. "What'd he do?

"Well," Chad laughs. "Jake ain't the smartest crayon in the box. He got drunk at the bar and on his way home, he thought he seen a deer in the field." Chad pauses as he chuckles and I have a hard time understanding him. "Wasn't a deer, though. It was old man Smith's pet llama."

My eyes go wide as I punch Chad in the stomach. "Shut up," I call out. "You're lying."

He raises his hand as he laughs loudly. "I swear it," he shouts. "That ain't the worst part."

I hang on to his words. How can it get any worse?

"Ole Jake felt real bad about it and tried to give the llama CPR," he laughs hysterically. "When deputy Paul showed up, he tried to pull him away, but he was dead set on saving its life. He punched Paul right in the face, so he's got assault charges to go along with it." Chad starts coughing and I'm shocked by his story. "I don't know what they're gonna do with him."

I'm blown away and can only shake my head as I pour creamer and sugar into my coffee and begin stirring. I can't help but laugh as I envision Jake giving the llama CPR. Jake is a nice guy. Stupid, but nice.

"Is there anyone else that can go?"

Chad shakes his head. "Nah. Everyone's tied up," he answers.

"Wait," I say as it hits me. "Don't they deliver?"

Chad laughs again. "They're parts truck is broke down. Ain't that funny? A parts company that has their parts truck broke down."

I don't laugh, only shrug my shoulders. It is a little funny, I guess, but not enough to get me to laugh.

"I'd be the one going if your mom or dad were here."

He pats me on the shoulder. "Sorry kiddo. That's what I need you to do."

"No worries," I admit, while putting a lid on my coffee. It's neat to do something that I've never done before. "I don't mind." I glance up at him. "What do I do?"

Chad laughs again as he explains to me where to go and who to talk to. I follow him to his desk and wait as he shuffles papers around before finally passing me one. "Give this to them. It has the part number to make it easier. They'll take care of everything."

I step to my desk and pick up my car keys.

"What're you doing?" he asks as he smiles at me. "It won't fit in your little bitty car. You need to take the parts truck."

I shrug my shoulders as I pass by him on my way toward the shop. How am I supposed to know how big a gas tank is? I guess I'll learn today.

The parts truck is dirty. Someone littered cigarette ashes everywhere, and the truck looks long overdue for a cleaning. When Jake gets out of jail, I'm going to make sure my father makes him clean this thing from top to bottom. This is not representative of our company.

The radio doesn't work, and neither does the air conditioner. I have both windows down and it's smoldering hot in here. I think the heat is making the smell even worse, and it's probably coming from all the trash piled on the passenger floorboard. I can't believe it's going to be so hot today. At least we'll get some relief when we get down to the creek. It's always fun down there. I just dread being the designated driver. Since I don't drink, they think I should always tote them around. Of course, I do it. I don't want any of them to get in an accident and hurt themselves. I would feel terrible about that.

I'm the only one in the group that doesn't drink. I've never touched the stuff and they never pressure me to. I still have a good time without it and I think they accept my choices. Ally drinks, but she doesn't go too far. She's my best friend in the group and our values align closer than the others. Our families go to the same church and have for as long as I can remember. We always get together for barbecues and game nights. She comes from a family steeped in Christian values, and I know her core beliefs are in line with mine. She just strays a little further from the Lord than I ever would. That's why I trust her when she laid out her plan to meet with Sam. I think the Lord might approve and I'm on board to try it. Although I don't believe Sam is actually going to repent, I trust in Ally. She's usually right about these things.

The parts store is on the opposite end of town and I'm roasting by the time I arrive. I can feel the dampness of sweat in my clothes and on the sides of my head. It's only a little after eight in the morning and I dread what heat the day will bring as it goes on. As I step out of the parts truck, I notice the sun is particularly bright. Although I'm hot, I'm thankful to have the clothing covering my skin. My fair complexion is easily burnt under these conditions, and I will need to ensure that I take extra precaution with sunscreen at the party this evening. I don't want to be burnt to a crisp when I go see my grandma. I really want to visit her and want nothing to disrupt that.

When I enter the store, I notice it's warm inside and feel no air moving at all. The man behind the counter smiles as he addresses me. "Good morning."

I step in front of him and place the paper on the counter. "I'm here to pick up a part."

He still smiles as he picks up the paper and lifts his glasses before looking over it. "Ah, yes," he exclaims. "We've got it ready for you. Sorry you had to come all the way over here. Damn parts truck is broken down."

I smile and nod as he continues. "Let me get

someone to help me. It's pretty heavy."

While he steps away, I glance at a display that showcases different keys and key rings. None are very pretty and most are made for men, I think.

The man returns to the counter, and I read his name tag. "Steve," I ask. "Is there a restroom around here?"

He glances down at his nametag and smiles as he points to his left. "Yes ma'am. Just right around the corner."

I smile as I turn toward the direction he points. Not far away, I see the restroom with a sign hanging in clear view. I feel a little embarrassed for having not looked around before asking. I'm better than that.

The store is hot, but the restroom is almost unbearable. The walls, made of concrete blocks, keep and magnify the heat. While I sit on the toilet, my backside and legs sweat and I slide a bit. Horrified by the thought of it, I finish quickly before washing my hands and stepping outside.

The stale air inside the store is almost pleasurable after being in the smoldering hot restroom. Steve is not at the counter when I return, so I step toward the window to peer outside, hoping to see them loading the part. I don't see anyone, and when I turn around, Steve approaches the counter once again.

"Sorry about the wait," he says. "My coworker is on the phone with her kid. It'll just be another moment."

"That's OK," I reply. "I'm in no hurry." I step back to the counter, where Steve and I fall silent. It's awkward, and he simply stares at me. I think about going outside, but I don't want to stand in the sun and get a burn. Finally, I break the ice. "It's hot in here. Is there something wrong with the air?"

Appearing happy to have me speak to him, he smiles widely. "Yeah," he answers. "Sorry about that. The air is broken and the guys can't be here until this afternoon."

"Goodness," I reply. "That'll be miserable for you. It's supposed to be a record-breaking day."

Steve nods. "Yes, it is," he returns before falling silent once again and we both stare at each other for a while. Eventually, he turns and disappears to the back for a moment before popping his head out.

"She's coming," he calls out. "How about you bring the truck over to the warehouse? That'll help get you out of here a little quicker."

I nod and step outside. I realize immediately how wrong I was about it being as hot inside as it is outside. At least there was a fan running inside. The sun is intensely hot and feels like it's just a few feet away. I climb into the truck and start the engine. After turning around, I slowly drive toward a building off to the side that I believe to be the warehouse. After scolding myself for not asking, I'm relieved to see Steve appear as he waves me forward, and I'm happy to see someone else climbing on a forklift. I'm ready to get out of this heat and back to the office.

After putting the truck in park, I step out, not knowing what I need to do. I'm not sure if I have to sign for it or if they'll just bill my father. Steve lowers the tailgate as I step to the rear of the truck. He motions for me to stand back as he climbs inside the bed and guides the operator to lift the bulky item. I see now why I couldn't bring my car. The thing is huge.

My eyes are on Steve as he slides the tank off and places it firmly in the bed. As the forklift operator reverses, I recognize her face immediately. It's Sam's mother, Karen. I did not know that she worked here. Horrified, I desire to get in the truck and leave before she spots me, but I can't. I don't know what I'm supposed to do.

Karen is a lovely woman and I feel ashamed of my thoughts about her. It's not her fault that Sam did what she did. She always treated me well when we were kids and I spent so much time around her it was like she was family. That all changed with Sam. I know she went to my parents, and the other parents, about when we disowned her, but it didn't do any good. It was mostly our parents that drove the separation. They just couldn't let us be a part of it, and I completely understand.

After she parks the forklift, she approaches the truck to help Steve as he works to strap the tank in the back. All at once, she recognizes me and turns toward me. I feel my cheeks go flush, and with my pale complexion, there's no hiding it.

"Hello Brooky," she calls out while grinning from ear to ear. "It's good to see you."

I smile awkwardly. "Hello Mrs. Walker."

"It's still Karen," she states as she strolls directly up to me and embraces me in a full, body to body hug. "How are you?"

I gently return her embrace, not knowing what else to do. "I'm good," I answer sheepishly. "And how are you?"

She releases me and places her hands on my shoulders as she looks me up and down. "I'm well," she answers while shaking her head. She steps back and her smile opens even brighter. "My, my, my," she continues. "Look at how much you've grown. You're such a beautiful young woman."

Unable to hide my discomfort, I can only smile as Steve closes the tailgate and steps next to us. I'm happy to have him join and turn my attention to him. "Do you need me to sign anything?" I ask.

Steve shakes his head. "Nah," he answers. "You're all set. Tell your dad I said hello."

I nod. "I will, and thank you very much." I turn back to Karen. "It was good to see you. Try to stay out of the heat."

She still smiles at me as I sidestep toward the truck. When I do, she takes a step closer.

"Are you ready for school to begin?" she asks.

"Yes," I answer. "I like school."

"I remember," she says. "You were always a good student and liked to play school with Sammy."

I smile. I remember that. I was always the teacher and got on to all the other kids all the time. I don't think they enjoyed it at all.

"Yeah," I admit. "That was fun." I open the door and slide in behind the seat. "Well, it was good to see you. I need to get this back to the shop. They're waiting for it."

Karen nods her head as she steps a little closer. "I understand," she replies. "It was good to see you, too."

As I start the truck, she continues. "Sammy told me he's going to meet you guys today. That's very nice of you and it makes me happy to have you guys back in our lives."

I smile and nod my head. "Me too," I lie before putting the truck in gear. "I really have to go, Mrs. Walker. My father says time is money."

She laughs and waves at me. "Have a good day, Brooky."

I return her wave as I pull away, being cautious that not to run over her feet. While glancing in the rearview mirror, I notice that she still waves and smiles at me. I pull onto the road and push on the accelerator. What an awkward encounter, and I think I made it worse.

I feel bad for Karen and wish I would've been more welcoming with her today. She is a lovely woman and always treated me well. Even after what I've done to her daughter, she speaks to me with such high regard. What a shame. The Christian in me wants to turn this truck around and hug her neck. I feel that she probably needs it. She lost as much as Sam did, and it wasn't her decision. Although I keep my eyes on the road, I speak a little prayer for Karen. I don't think the Lord will mind.

When I finish my prayer, my thoughts turn to Sam

and our get together this afternoon. My stomach churns at the thought of it, and I hate the idea of going. While I miss her, I'm ashamed of her and what she's become. She's blasphemous and nothing more than a walking sin. I must speak with her and guide her back to the light. I pray that I'm strong enough to do so.

Thinking back to our childhood, I can't help but smile as I remember our group, running around together and always looking after one another. Sam was always so awkward, but there was a light that glowed in her soul. I remember the way she was with animals and how we dreamed of being veterinarians together. I remember the way she cared for every member of our group. How she thought of them. The way she talked so highly of them behind their back. If one of us came down sick, she would have her mom bring her by with some soup and she'd pray over them.

How can such a lovely person grow into the sinner I see now? It just doesn't seem right. A person can't just change overnight and expect everyone to get used to it. Especially with what she's asking for. She should be ashamed of herself.

While parking the truck back at the shop, I can't help but feel relieved. I get to stay in the air conditioning and get some much needed work done. Since I'm leaving early, I feel energetic and want to get as much done as I can. I don't want my father thinking I turned lazy because of the short workday. I want to make him proud.

Caden Astor

It's insanely hot and I'm drenched from head to toe in sweat. Barely able to brave it any longer, I jog down to the creek and kick my shoes off. Being one that enjoys every opportunity to carry my pistol, I pull it from my waistband and tuck it in my shoe. Not only do I keep it in my Jeep at all times, I always have it on me when I'm at the cabin, alone. I don't like the thought of anyone or anything creeping up on me, and I hope to at least have a fighting chance. Sometimes, I just walk around and shoot old bullfrogs or random trees to improve my accuracy. No one is ever around to hear it, and I know my father won't miss it when he's gone.

After pulling my tank top from over my head, I walk toward the water. Using caution, I step lightly as tiny pebbles stab and burn at the bottom of my feet, causing immediate sensation. When I reach shin depth, I feel the heat release from my body as the cold water drives away the exhaustion. Knowing that a deeper pool is just ahead, I shudder with anticipation as I dive headfirst into the water and emerge quickly.

"Hell yeah!" I scream aloud, even though no one is around to hear me.

Feeling refreshed with the quick dip, I know I need to return to work. I've got a party to prepare for and I want it to be epic. I'd love nothing more than to take my fishing pole and walk this creek for the rest of the day, but it'll have to wait.

Once again, I step slowly as I climb out of the creek and sit down on the gravel bar to put on my shoes. The rocks are hot and burn my butt, but the water from my shorts quickly cools everything and I feel the heat dwindling on my backside as I lace my sneakers.

When I finish, I take a moment to view my surroundings. This spot of the creek is sweltering under the hot summer sun, but it is a beautiful place. The cabin is simple and we don't have any power out here, but the land is breath-taking. My grandpa owns fifty acres, surrounding me on every side, and it is prime land for both hunting and fishing. With my father being in such poor health, I know he won't be able to take it when my grandpa dies and it'll be all mine. I hope that's not for a long time, though. I love my grandpa and will miss him when he's gone.

Grandpa was a marine in Vietnam and is a tough ole bird. He is my idol, plain and simple. When he came home from the war, he worked for an oilman in Texas until he started prospecting on his own. His oil business was successful, but was nothing compared to his other investments. After moving here from Texas, he put most of his money into energy and lumped other investments into tech companies. I don't know how he knew they were going to be big, but he did. He made crazy money and, in return, invested that money into the energy field. Our family still has a stake in some oil wells in Texas, Oklahoma, and Kansas, but the biggest thing we have going anymore is with renewable resources and wind energy. My grandpa and dad have built a large wind turbine business and operate on almost every farm for a hundred miles in every direction. I just wish my father could stay around to keep the business going when grandpa dies. I have no desire to run the business, I just want to spend the money.

My dad was a marine, just like my grandpa. He's my hero too and I love the man with all my heart. They want me to join the marines, just like them, but I don't want to. I figure to get a football scholarship and I hope to join a fraternity and party like my life depends on it.

My father is who I get my athletic ability from. He was a hell of an athlete and could've played division one, but he met my mom in high school and that was it. He went off to the Marine Corps, and they got married shortly after. When his service ended, he moved home and worked his way through college, while learning the business from grandpa. He's done some big things to grow the company and I think the wind energy stuff was mostly his idea. I'm not completely sure, but I think so.

It sucks that he's sick and it'll tear me apart when he dies. He has colon cancer and things have gotten rough for him. I don't think he'll make it much longer. Grandpa told me to make sure I take care of him while he's gone on the cruise and I have, mostly. I just can't miss an opportunity to throw a banger at the creek with grandpa out of town. It's gonna be sick!

I think that both my grandpa and my dad know that I'm not capable of running their big business. I'm simply not smart enough. I try, but it's just not a part of me and I love to party. I love hanging out with people and meeting new ones. Grandpa says I need to buckle down and smarten up, but I don't really want to. I'm going to marry Ally and she can run the business. She's definitely smart enough to do it and we'd be better off to have her in charge. I'll just be her little love bunny. That way, I can play golf, and hunt, and fish all day before I love her up in the evening time. It's the best idea I have ever had and I'll stand by it.

Standing to my feet, I dust off the bottom of my shorts and pick up my tank top and pistol. Not wanting to add any more insulation to my body, I toss my shirt over my shoulder and carry the pistol in hand as I return toward the cabin. At six foot four, I'm able to cover a lot of ground. I'm toned, with barely any body fat, but I'm built slim and quick as a wink. That's what makes me tough on the football field. Well, that and the fact that I can throw the football a quarter mile. I've got the best arm in the state and have the next two years to show everyone what I can do.

As I step onto the porch, I toss my shirt in the chair and place the gun firmly on top. I don't want to be far from my weapon, but I can't keep it in my wet shorts. It might slip out and drop to the ground. I wouldn't like that. After noticing a smudge on the barrel, I extend my arm to wipe it off to ensure it's not scratched. As I do, I catch a glimpse of my arm. My tan is dark and I love it. I've been running around without a shirt for most of the summer and it shows. I noticed this morning that my blonde hair is lighter and my blue eyes shine brighter with this dark tan. I'm killing it on Instagram with my pictures. Many girls comment and like my pictures. Poor things. They'll never understand how much I love Ally. No matter what comes along, I wouldn't do anything to hurt my Ally girl. I'm all hers, and for as long as she wants me, which I hope is forever.

Getting back to work, I drag log after log to the gravel bar to prepare for the giant bonfire I have in mind. I wish Brock was here to help me, but he needed to work today. It would suck to be poor, like him, and need to work when you are supposed to be enjoying your youth. I'll never make my son do that. I'll make sure he experiences life.

Brock is my best friend, and I love him dearly. I hate the idea of him going off to college next year and leaving me. I still have another year after he leaves, and I'm going to miss him. I hope he gets a scholarship somewhere I want to go, so I can join him and we can play together again. I know it's a longshot, but that's what I hope for. I know Ally is following me, and I wish Millie and Brooke would also. It would be awesome for us to all stick together.

I can't help but worry about Brock. Although he is always distant and negative, there was something really wrong with him this morning. He just didn't act right at all. He was cold and didn't laugh at a single one of my jokes. That's not like him. He might be a serious man, but he has a healthy sense of humor and I was killing it today. I was bashing on everyone, and it was good stuff. I certainly hope he lightens up before tonight. I want him and everyone else to have a good time at my party. I love the dude.

Getting everything else ready for the party is a breeze. I've got beer in the coolers, just need to get ice on my way back out here. There's liquor and mixers for the partiers, and water for the losers. I hope Brooke brings her own drink because I didn't even think of her. I guess I can stop at the store and pick her up something if she doesn't.

The speakers are set up, and I've already tested them. They're loud and perfect for the party I have planned. I borrowed them from the school. They won't mind as long as they never find out. I should be able to return them before anyone needs them. Nobody is really around the school right now, other than coaches and football players. The cheerleaders meet across town at an indoor facility since it's been so hot lately. Surely Brock and I can slip them back in with no one noticing. If not, my grandpa will get me out of it. He always has my back.

After checking my phone, I notice that it's getting late. Not wanting to be tardy for Ally, I climb onto the porch and grab my pistol, tucking it securely in the band of my shorts as I free up my hands to pull the tank top over my head. I pull the door to the cabin closed, but don't lock it. No one is going to come out here, and the only reason I'm closing the door is to keep the wild animals out. Otherwise, the air flow would make the place cooler if anyone should want to hang in there tonight. I don't know why they would, but I don't mind. I'm going to have a mess to clean up anyway and one more thing won't matter.

As I climb into my Jeep, I hear someone call my name out from somewhere behind me. I think it's coming from down by the creek. Knowing that I'm all alone out here, and there's not a house even remotely close, I'm horrified when I turn to see Brock. He's shirtless and running along the gravel bar. His face appears ghastly, and without hesitation, I sprint toward him. After pulling my pistol, I click the safety off and point it at the ground as I run toward him and search for whatever might be chasing.

"Caden," he cries out. "Don't leave me!"

Worried, I run for him and become troubled when he collapses to his knees just as I reach his side. His chest heaves uncontrollably as he breathes heavily and he appears exhausted.

"What the hell?" I yell. "Are you alright? Where did you come from?"

He glances up at me while sucking at air. "I beat the hell out of Rob," he wheezes. "I beat him real bad."
Unable to comprehend, I can't help but ask. "Who the hell is Rob?"

He shakes his head as he works to catch his breath, and I wait patiently. I kneel next to him and rub his shoulder. While he works to gain air, I notice his hand is wrapped in his shirt and there's blood showing through. I tuck my gun back in the band of my shorts before reaching down and lifting his arm. I unwrap the shirt from his hand. I'm completely blown away to see his blood-stained knuckles, cut and damaged, with fragments of skin hanging loosely. My mouth falls open and I stare at him blankly.

"He made a joke," he pants heavily. He swallows harshly, and I hear the dryness of his throat. "He made a joke about Sam."

I turn to sit on my backside and listen as he tells me what happened and what he did. His breathing eases and I see him relax a little. I feel bad for him. I know how he felt about Sam and I know he's been struggling with his anger lately. I listen intently and rub his shoulder as he talks. I hope to help ease his stress. I will always be here for him and I hope he knows that.

"OK, I know what we're going to do," I announce once he finishes. "I don't want to bother my dad with this. He has a treatment in the city and won't be back until late. You can stay here at the cabin until grandpa gets home. He'll be back on Sunday and he'll know what to do."

"You don't understand," he says, worried. "I beat him really bad. I may have killed him."

I smile, hoping to calm him as I nod toward his hand. "I see that," I reply. "But I doubt you killed him. It's just an assault, and I think you were probably justified."

"I don't know," he continues. "He was having a seizure, I think."

I laugh out loud. "That's nothing. I see fights like that on Instagram all the time. Give me your phone," I say as I reach my hand out. "I'll show you."

He looks up at me and shakes his head. "Lost it. I think I left it on the table at the diner."

I nod my head and exhale. "No worries. I have a spare you can have." I reach down and help him to his feet. "Go wash up in the creek and I'll get you some clothes. It'll make you feel better."

Without waiting for a response, I jog to the cabin and disappear inside. I find a bar of soap and the first aid kit before grabbing a pair of my swim trunks and a brand new tank top. I was going to wear them tonight at the party, but Brock needs them more. Maybe I'll swing by the house and get another set, if I have time.

I jog back outside and find him still standing where I left him. "Come on man," I call out. "Get cleaned up. We gotta go." I toss him the soap and watch as he catches it, but stares at me curiously.

"What? Where are we going?"

I smile at him, figuring he forgot in all the chaos. "We have to meet Sam."

"I'm not going to that," he returns and I see his anger returning. "I'm staying here."

I inhale deeply and place my arm on his shoulder. "It'll only take a minute and they'll never find you in my Jeep. We're just picking up the girls before going to the fort. No one will ever think to look there." I smile for him. "I bet they're not even looking for you. He probably didn't even say anything."

"Man," he replies. "I don't want to go to jail."

I study Brock and I think he's about to cry. I don't like to see him scared like this, and I don't want him to worry. We can fix it. My grandpa will get him out of it.

"It ain't that big of a deal," I say. "It'll all be OK. Grandpa will take care of it." I open my smile even broader as I prepare to tell him a lie to trick him into coming with me. "Plus, you don't want to stay here right now. Grandpa has a conservation agent scheduled to inspect the land today. They work closely with the police and you don't want to be here when he comes out."

"Why would a conservation agent come out here?" he asks.

I shrug my shoulders and try to keep the lie small. "Not real sure," I answer. "Something to do with permits." I watch his facial expression change and feel like he's worried about it. "And you promised Ally you would be there today." I add and notice his face relax a bit as his eyes dart back and forth.

"I don't want to go to jail," he repeats.

I have him, and I know it. "You're not going to jail," I assure him. "I'll drive careful and it won't take long."

Before he has a chance to respond, I drop the clothes and first aid kit to the ground before turning and jogging back to the cabin. "Get cleaned up. I forgot to get you a towel."

I cross the floor and grab a towel from the closet. When I return to the doorway, I stop as I watch him take his pants off and wade out in the water while only wearing his boxers. I pick up my phone from the table and pull up Ally's contact.

"Brock beat the hell out of some guy and he's goin' to have to stay at the cabin tonight. I talk him into going with me, but he's real angry now. I don't know how to help him."

I return to the gravel bar and wait patiently while he finishes up. As he dresses, my phone dings back from my pocket. It's Ally.

"Oh no. I'll pray for him. Take care of him and I'll see you later."

"OK."

Once he's fully dressed, we patch his hand with what supplies we have available. I think it looks pretty good, even though we used too much gauze and his hand appears like it's in a cast. We eventually load into my Jeep and I feel the handle of the pistol digging into my skin. After pulling it from my waistband, I pass it to Brock.

"Will you toss this in the glove box, please?"

He takes it from me and turns it over and over in his hand as he stares at it blankly. Brock knows I carry a pistol with me and he enjoys shooting guns, too. I think he's a better shot than I am, and when my father passes, I'm going to give him one of his own. He'll like that, I think.

As he places the gun in the glove box, I put the Jeep in drive and make my way down the driveway. I glance over at Brock and can't help but think he looks pretty good in my clothes. I don't think his own clothes fit him right and I probably need to help him shop.

"The clothes fit you nice," I say.

He looks down and nods his head before looking up and staring out the windshield. "Text my brother and let him know where I'm at," he requests, without even looking at me or mentioning the clothes. "He won't tell anyone, and I know he's worried about me."

I watch him for another moment as he simply stares out the window. Doing as he asks, I pull my phone out and text Blake to let him know his brother is OK. As I slide my phone under my leg, I keep watch on Brock, but he never glances at me. He only stares out the window and appears to me like a beat dog. My heart hurts for him.

The driveway is long and curvy, but I know it like the back of my hand, so I drive the Jeep at unsafe speeds. I'm not afraid and I always get a thrill from it. When I reach the gate, I leave it open and turn out to the highway, heading back into town. I need to remember to bring the balloons when I return. That's how I plan to mark the entrance, so everyone knows where to turn.

The drive into town isn't far. It's only a few miles. The Jeep is loud and air blows inside from all directions with the top off. It may be hot, but I think it feels fantastic as the air pounds at my body. I reach down and feel that my shorts are already dry. Maybe not completely, but what remains is most likely caused by sweat. As I lift my hand to my face, I notice a bruise on my forearm and remember hitting it on the helmet of that grizzly bear that tackled me at practice this morning. I thought Brock was going to kill him. His anger really is out of control lately and I hope he gets it together.

Coach had us all come in early this morning for practice, since it was going to be so hot out today. He says we're all babies and thinks the entire world is full of softies since he has to cater to us to ensure we don't get too hot. I'm no softy. I would practice whenever he told me to. I ain't no baby, that's for sure.

I reach in the back seat and fiddle with the cooler as I pull out a beer. I pass one to Brock and smile when I see him open it and take a long drink. He probably needs it, I think. After popping mine open, I have a sip and again think back to Brock's attitude lately. I really wish he'd stop being so aggressive all the time and cut the negativity. I hope he's not going through his depression again. He struggles with that stuff and I feel bad for him. I know he had it rough with his dad, and growing up poor, but I don't know how to help him. I just try to help him have a good time and listen if he wants to talk, which is almost never. He's quiet, even around me sometimes, and I've been his best friend since forever. He's just a different kind of person. Maybe he needs to get laid, I think. I'll see if I can hook him up tonight. Maybe that'll help cure his case of the blues.

I pull my phone out and scroll through the group message. I chuckle to myself in knowing Brock won't see it, but I don't want to start a new thread and I think the girls will worry about him if he's not in it.

"I'm on my way to get you. Millie be at your house in five minutes."

After sending the message, I pull up Ally's contact, since she never texted me back.

"I love you and hope you feel better soon."
"I'll come get you after we meet with Sam."
Smiling at the thought of her, I slide my phone

under my leg and take another swallow of beer. I love my Ally girl. She's the best thing that ever happened to me and I can't wait to spend the rest of my life with her. She's my best friend and always knows what's best for me. Hell, she knows what's best for everyone. She's a Christian woman and smarter than anyone I've ever known. She's loving, forgiving, and caring, but she can be mean when she needs to. When a tough thing needs said or done. She'll do it and pray on it later. I've never been one for God and religion, but I'm coming around. The way Ally tells it, it's much better than any way I've ever heard it before.

When Ally and I get married, I'm going to fill her house with children. She wants a big family, and she's close to hers. I just have my little brother and I love the guy, but he just wants to cramp my style. I might appreciate him later in life, but right now, he drives me nuts.

Ally's not like that with her siblings. She loves them all the time and will do anything for them. To be honest, she'll do anything for anyone. Her heart has been on Sam lately. When she told me her plan, I didn't even second guess it. If she wants to make up with him, that's OK with me. I miss him too and wouldn't mind having him back in the group. Even if it gets a little weird.

I pull to a stop in front of Millie's house and honk the horn. I grab my phone under my leg before finishing the last swallow of beer and toss the can in the back seat. Looking at my screen, I see the others text me back, but I only open Ally's.

"Love you too." Is all that it reads.

"See you soon."

I hate that she's struggling with Sam. I'll be glad when this is over and she feels better about things. Sam will come around and Ally will be alright. It'll all work out in the end.

"You couldn't pull into the driveway?" Millie calls

out as she opens the door.

I glance in her direction and laugh as she climbs in the back seat and lays her bag at her feet. "Didn't think about it," I answer honestly.

She shakes her head. "Hello Brock," she announces.

Brock turns in his seat. "You want the front?"

"Nah," she answers. "I'm going to sit in back with Brooke. She wants some pointers for a workout. Says she needs to lose some weight."

I smile after hearing her say it. Brooke's not that big, but I applaud anyone for trying to get in better shape. Healthiness is the key to happiness, I believe. "Pass me a beer, please. Brock, you need one?"

"Sure," he says. "I can use one."

Millie leans over and I hear her fish around in the ice. I put the Jeep in gear and pull away when I feel the sting of the cold can as she lays it on my shoulder. I jump and snatch it from her hand. "Thanks."

I glance at Brock and watch him open the can before tilting it to the sky and probably finishing most of it. He needs to chill if he's going to make it to the party. I pop open my can and reach it out to him. "Cheers," I mutter.
His face is stern and void of emotion. After he bumps my can, he swallows the rest and tosses it to the floor.

"Thanks Millie," I repeat, hoping she catches I appreciate it.

She doesn't respond, and as I drive toward Brooke's house, I glance in the rearview mirror and see that she already has her phone out. She's leaned back and snapping photos as she contorts her face from silly smiles to pouty lips.

Millie is pretty, but nothing compared to my Ally. There's a fakeness about her that makes her less appealing and she's always been that way. She has a super-hot body, but when she removes the makeup, you can see all the acne scars and discoloration. I still remember her as a young kid, with pimples everywhere, and she definitely wasn't pretty. She's come a long way. However, I don't think the makeup makes her unattractive, I just prefer women to remain natural. Nobody needs that much makeup. It's her personality that makes her so unattractive to me. She's a bitch and proud of it. If she doesn't have your back, look out. She'll shame you to no end, unless you have clout. Then she'll go along with anything you say. Well, that's as long as it boosts her social status. She has a huge Instagram following and I think it'll grow even larger when she gets out of here and moves to a big city. I think she's destined for great things. She just knows how to go along and make things work for her benefit. I love her though and wouldn't change a single thing about her.

"What?"

I glance back to see her staring at me blankly. When I realize she never heard me, I have to laugh at her one-track mind. Sure, she's smarter than me, but she only focuses on herself. Nothing else matters.

"Nothing," I answer as I pull into Brooke's driveway.

She's sitting on a porch swing and stands as I come to a stop. Brooke is always ready, but in this heat, I would've waited in the air conditioning.

"I see how it is," Millie speaks up. "You'll pull in the driveway so miss Brooky doesn't have to walk, but you make me hike all the way to the curb."

"I pulled in her driveway because you got onto me," I laugh. "You want me to back out and make her walk to the curb?"

"Well, no," she answers. "I'm just saying."

I laugh again as Brooke tosses her bag in the back before climbing in the seat next to Millie. "What's up, Brooke?"

Brooke shakes her head and I see the sweat beaded along her forehead. "Nothing. It's hot!"

"We'll get cooled off soon," I respond as I take a sip of beer. "I was in the creek earlier and it was awesome."

"Caden Astor!" Brooke calls out. "Let me drive if you're going to drink. You're not putting our lives at risk." I laugh out loud as I glance at her in the mirror. Her face is serious and I know she means business. "I've only had one, I promise."

"Still," she replies. "I'm not riding with you if you're going to be drinking. It's against the law."

"Fine," I say. "I won't drink." I lift the can and take a long drink, almost finishing the rest. I belch as I pass it across to Brock, who finishes what's left. "Happy?"

She wrinkles her nose while Millie lets out a chuckle. "I'd be happier if you ever got any manners." She reaches up and taps Brock on the shoulder. "Hey Brock."

Brock simply nods and tosses the empty can on the floor at his feet. He turns his head in all directions while looking around and appears to me like an inmate who escaped from prison.

I continue laughing and can't help but think about what a weird bunch we are, before eventually putting the Jeep in reverse and pulling out of the driveway. As I glance behind me, I watch as Millie throws her arm around Brooke and lifts the camera to their faces.

"Smile bitch," she cheerfully calls out and I watch their faces widen with smiles, only to quickly diminish once Millie snaps the photo.

I crank the volume on the radio and race off, lurching them all back in their seats. I smile as I glance at Brock to see his reaction. Nothing. He simply stares forward, out the window, showing no emotion.

"Slow down," Brooke calls out. "Are you sure you don't want me to drive?"

I don't answer, but follow her request and slow to a reasonable speed. I don't want to get Brock picked up, anyway. I can see that he's clearly concerned with the situation he's in, and I don't think he wants to talk right now. I know how he is and it'll take a while before he eases up. I think he needs a little while to cool off and maybe he'll realize it's not that bad. I feel bad for Brock and I know he doesn't know what to do. His father left them in a tight spot and his mom isn't much help. He's poor and doesn't have a lot of options. He doesn't have anywhere to go and no way to get there. He doesn't have a car and needs his job to get by. He wanted to get as many hours in as he could since summer is almost over and he's trying to stack up some cash. I hope my grandpa can save his job after beating that guy up. But if anyone can do it, it's my grandpa.

I don't know where to go, but I figure I need to kill a little time before we go to the park. It won't be good for this crew to be standing around, waiting for Sam to get there. Brock may take off on me, and the other two will do nothing but complain about the heat.

The wind blows through the open top and feels great. The knobby tires are loud on the road and mixes with the airflow and loud music. I hear the girls talking loudly to one another, but I can't make out what they say. I ease the throttle faster, hoping to slip it in without Brooke noticing as I start singing at the top of my lungs. I'm not a very good singer, but I don't care. I love this song.

I pick up my phone and notice a message from Ally.

"Are you there yet? How's Sam acting?"

"Not there yet. Driving around for a minute. Ready to get this over with so we can party."

"OK."

Disappointed by her response, I text back. *"How you feeling?"*

Ally replies and I read it from the lock screen.

"Better. See you there."

I pull my phone out of my pocket and have to swerve to keep from hitting a cat. I sigh aloud and I'm very thankful not to have run over the poor kitty. I open the message to reply. *"Good deal. Love you,"* and hit send before immediately noticing that I sent it to Brock's phone. I laugh when I catch my error and send a follow-up message. *"Sorry. Meant for Ally."*

I pull up her contact. *"Good deal. Love you."*

I laugh out loud and stick my phone back under my leg as I turn to look at Brock, hoping he finds humor in it.

"What's so funny?" Millie asks.

"I accidentally told Brock I love him," I answer, glancing in the rearview. "It was supposed to go to Ally."

Brooke laughs as Millie piles on. "Knew it. Knew you guys were too close to just be bros."

I laugh again, but Brock just stares ahead. I want him to joke with me, but he won't. Not sure how I sent that to him, but I can't help to think that I do, in fact, love Brock. I love them all, we just don't say it to each other.

"I saw Sam today," Millie continues. "He was outside of Ally's daycare."

I turn in my seat as Brooke speaks up. "I saw Karen today at the parts store."

"No way," I reply and watch as Brock turns to look at them as well. "That's weird," I continue. "I thought he didn't get out much."

Brock listens but doesn't speak. Although his face appears angry, I still think he looks like he's going to cry. How does a person look angry and about to cry at the same time? I wonder.

I turn back to face her. "How was he?"

Millie shakes her head. "Didn't stop." She puffs out her cheeks and widens her hands around her belly. "Bro is fat, though."

"He was fat at the end of the school year," I speak up. "You saying he's bigger?"

"Oh yeah," she nods before puffing her cheeks out again.

"Karen looks like she's twenty years older," Brooke interjects. "All of this must've been hard on her."

I glance back toward Brooke and can't help but think that she looks a little teary-eyed, as well. "How is Karen?" I ask. "I always liked her."

"Me too," Millie adds. "She was a nice person."

"I didn't talk to her for very long," Brooke answers. "But she gave me a hug and wanted to know what I've been up to." She sighs aloud. "She's still a nice person."

"Can we go?" Brock barks at me. "I don't want to talk about them."

"Jeez," Brooke replies. "Just telling you, I saw her."

"Sorry," he apologizes. "I just don't want to talk about them. It's bad enough that we're going to see him and try to make friends again. It's just weird."

I turn to look at Brock as he speaks. He his face appears even angrier now, and he again stares out the window again, not looking at me or anyone.
"Can we go?" he repeats. "I wanna get this over with and I need another drink."

I laugh as I nod and continue forward. I sure hope he gets in a better mood soon. He better not bring this negativity to my party. I don't really want to do this either, but we have to. Ally said that it's for the best.

I crank the music as I pull out onto the street. I hear Millie and Brooke singing from the back seat and I join in. While glancing over at Brock, I notice his jaw muscles tighten and he appears to be biting hard. I think he looks far too angry to be an eighteen-year-old kid. No one should look that angry at his age.

I reach out and tap him on the shoulder. When he

turns toward me, I mouth the word, "Chill."

He inhales deeply and I see his face relax. He nods his head and forces a smile. I'll take it, I think to myself. Negative Nelly over there needs to chill.

As I speed through town, I feel happy while we sing together, and even Brooke dances in the back seat. If I can get Brock to have a good time, then we'll really be partying. I drive past Ally's house and only slow down as I blow through the stop sign at the end of the street, not far from the park. Brock reaches over and turns the music off. I'm still singing as he speaks.

"You drove right by Ally's house," he says. "Are you already drunk?"

I smile at him, thinking that he saw how many beers I had. "Nah," I answer. "She's not feeling good. She'll be here soon."

His face goes blank. "What?" he calls out. "This was her damn idea."

"Relax man," I reply as I pull up alongside the curb. "She's coming. She just said to get started without her and she will be here." I shut the Jeep off and look around but don't see Sam. Maybe he's at the fort already.

"This is bullshit!" he shouts. "I didn't want to come. Just take me home."

"She should be here," Millie adds. "He's right. This was her idea."

I nod at them and blow heavily through my lips. "Yes," I agree. "And, I said she's coming. Her stomach hurts, and she's going to be a little late, is all." I twist in my seat as I make eye contact with each of them. "She'll be here."

"This is bullshit," Brock repeats as he pounds the dashboard.

Brooke speaks up. "Brock. What happened to your hand?"

Brock's face drops, and he looks like he doesn't

know what to say. "He hurt it at work today," I answer for him.

"Awe," Millie and Brooke mutter in unison as Brock glances toward me, appearing thankful.
Brooke pats him on the shoulder. "I'll pray that it heals quickly," she says.

Brock turns back to look out the window and I chuckle to myself as I think about his predicament. "It'll be alright," I assure them. "It's just a little flesh wound."

I drive forward the short distance to the park and hear him grumbling something to himself. I can't help but smile. He's an angry person, but I love him and he's just having a terrible day. After pulling alongside the curb, I put the Jeep in park and jump out. I hear the ding from my phone and glance down. It's Ally.

"I'm coming now. I'm feeling better and I will see you. Wait there for me."

"OK."

I glance up and see her a couple of blocks away. She's near her house, but she's walking down the sidewalk. "See," I say to the others while pointing in her direction. "She's right there."

I feel something squishy on my feet. I peek down to see I'm standing in a fresh pile of vomit. I wipe my shoe across the grass. Gross.

"Someone puked," I call out. "I wonder if it was fat Sam?"

Ally Carpenter

As the alarm clock sounds on my phone, I glance over to notice that it's still dark outside. After picking up my phone, I silence the alarm and roll to my back. Without hesitation, I scroll downward and open the text message alert. What a surprise. Another late-night message from Caden.

"I luv u mor than anything in the wurld."

I laugh and feel somewhat proud that he actually spelled 'anything' right. Although, I'm not exactly sure how someone can send a message with such poor grammar when they have auto-correct. He must have it turned off, I think, and I'll need to remember to turn it back on for him. That's just embarrassing.

"I love you too," I reply.

Almost immediately, my phone dings back with his response and I'm surprised he's up at this hour. It's only six in the morning and he usually sleeps in.

"I love yu more."

"Why are you up so early?" I question.

"Goofball practice."

"Football practice," he corrects.

I laugh as I place my phone on the nightstand. I don't want to get into a big deal and I remember now that they changed football practice too early this morning because of the heat. This boy won't stop texting and I always need to end our conversations. He constantly needs to send the last message and I don't understand why. It doesn't matter what it is, he must have the last word.

I toss the covers from my body and stand up before sliding my slippers on. Scurrying to the bathroom, I feel as if I'm going to wet myself. After barely making it, I plop down on the toilet and rub at my eyes, helping them adjust to the light. I enjoy rising early in the morning and don't mind that it's my turn to cook. At least my little brother will help me, and I think we'll do a fair job.

After washing my hands, I cut out the light and make my way down the hall. I lightly tap on Tyler's door before pushing it open, only to find him still in bed. I step beside him and gently wiggle his shoulder.

"Tyler," I whisper. "It's time to get up."

Tyler rolls over and blinks his eyes open before sitting upright. As he starts to rub his eyes, I feel that he's awake and return to the door.

Our stairs are old and creaky, so I take my time, hoping not to wake the others. I'm the oldest of four children, with each of us separated by only a year, give or take a month. My parents always wanted a large family and I think they were a little disappointed that they had to stop at four. I don't know exactly what stopped them, but I heard there was an issue with the last pregnancy that prompted the doctor to talk them into stopping. I wouldn't care if there were ten more. I love each of my siblings, and the more, the merrier.

After walking into the kitchen, I flip the light on and begin pulling ingredients from the refrigerator and placing them on the counter. As a family of six, we take turns cooking breakfast so that everyone gets a chance to sleep in. We always cook in pairs and it works out seamlessly. Since Tyler and I are the oldest, we team together while our parents each take one of our younger siblings. Tyler and I are a good pair. We never argue, and each of us knows our role and work together to complete the task. My father's breakfasts are always the best because he's the best cook and likes to get creative. You never know what he's going to make. This morning, we're going to prepare scrambled eggs with bacon and toast. We have it quite a bit, but none of us mind. It's a good breakfast.

As I finish pulling the last of the ingredients from the refrigerator, Tyler yawns loudly while walking to the cabinet. After getting a cup, he sticks it under the faucet and turns it to his mouth, drinking the whole thing in one swallow. Not seeming to be satisfied, he repeats the process once more, before pulling two skillets out of the cabinet and placing them on the stove. He clicks the fire on for each burner and steps next to me before picking up two packets of bacon.

"What'd you do last night?" he asks.

I crack eggs into a mixing bowl. "Went to a party at Madison's," I answer. "Brooke brought me home pretty early. Where were you?"

As he lines bacon in the pan, he shakes his head. "Here. I just stayed in my room all night playing video games. Didn't feel like going out."

"Don't you have football practice this morning?" I ask.

"Yeah, but I don't have to be there until seven. I can still help and take my breakfast with me."

I add an entire dozen eggs to the bowl, pour in some

half and half, and a few dashes of salt and pepper before beginning to whisk. "Are you going to Caden's tonight?" I question.

He nods his head as he forks at a slice of bacon. "Yeah," he answers before turning toward me with a smile. "Is Millie gonna be there?"

I stop whisking and turn toward him, pointing with the gelatinous end of the whisk. "No!" I exclaim. "She's too old for you."

He laughs aloud. "Nah, she's just right. I like older women."

While still pointing with the whisk, I can't help but smile and continue. "She'll eat you alive. You can't handle Millie."

After a good laugh from each of us, we carry on with conversation as we cook breakfast. As always, we wash the dishes as we go, never leaving a mess to the end. The toast is the easiest part and we usually save it for last. In record time, we have everything placed on the table when the first family member arrives.

"Good morning, children," my father announces as he pulls a coffee cup out of the cabinet and fills it from the pot. "The food smells delicious, and that bacon was making my nose dance."

I laugh as I place a stack of plates on the table and take a seat. I watch as my mother enters, followed by my younger brother and baby sister. She walks directly to my father and kisses him on the cheek before filling her own cup of coffee and doctoring it with creamer from the refrigerator.

"The food smells delicious," she echoes my father. "Tyler, where are you going?"

I look up to see my brother exiting the kitchen. "Getting my bag," he answers from over his shoulder while continuing to walk. "I'll be right back."

I glance at my mother. "He has football practice this morning. They moved it on account of the heat."

My mother nods as my father chimes in. "Good lord. They're teaching them to play flag football, aren't they? A little heat won't hurt them."

My mother playfully slaps him on the arm. "Stop it, Jim. It's supposed to be extremely hot today. They say it's going to break the record."

"Still," he persists. "Back in my day, we would've had football practice and I would've thrown hay bales until the sun went down. A little heat never killed anyone."

"I think the doctors would disagree," she replies before turning her attention to me. "Did you sleep well, honey?"

I nod and smile. "Yes, I did," I answer. "Did you?"

She sighs. "Somewhat. It's tough with this big bear snoring in my ear. It'll teach me not to read late and let him get to sleep before me."

My father is unfazed by her comment and glances up as Tyler returns. He drops his bag near the entryway and approaches the table.

"I have football practice this morning," he says as he folds out a napkin and places two pieces of toast next to each other.

"That's what Ally said," my father replies. "I guess they're moving their schedule so you sissies aren't out in the heat."

My brother simply smiles as he spoons a heaping portion of eggs onto the toast and adds bacon to the pile. After slapping the other piece of toast over the top, I notice he's made a sandwich and smile as he folds it up in the napkin. Smart, I think. He kisses my mother on the cheek before patting my father on the shoulder. "See ya," he mutters while turning on his heels.

"Hold on, cowboy," my father calls out. "We'll say

grace while you're still here."

We all bow our heads as my father speaks a blessing over our food. When he finishes, my brother scoots across the floor and picks up his bag on his way out the door.

For the rest of breakfast, we visit with each other, staying current with what's happening in each of our lives. We are a close family, aligned with Christian morals and led by my father, who sets a great example for the rest of us. He's a hard-working man who focuses on faith, family, and this community. My father has been a banker for my entire life and my mother works closely beside him. We have money, but I don't know how much. We've never gone without, but we're not extravagant. My father has the same fishing boat that my grandpa had and a lawnmower that barely starts, let alone runs. I swear the man is going to have a heat stroke trying to get it started one of these days.

We're all active members of our community church and strive to help those in need. Although I am steeped in Christianity, I also take part in some of the sinfulness of our nation's youth. I drink but don't do drugs. I cuss sometimes, but never in front of people. I have sex, but only with Caden, and I don't think that counts. We're already promised to one another and only await graduation to make it official in the eyes of the Lord. When I drink, I keep it on an even keel and won't allow myself to get carried away. My plan is to drink through college and quit once I marry Caden so we can start a family. I want to experience life, just not at the risk of my ever after.

Following breakfast, I excuse myself and return to my bedroom for my clothes. I like to be first to shower so I get the hottest water. The water heater never seems to make it through all of us, and I feel a little greedy this morning.

After removing my clothes, I step into the shower and lather up. The hot water pounds at my skin and feels invigorating. I step closer, climbing to my tiptoes and allow the water to massage my face. I am excited about today. I prepared a bible lesson for the children at the daycare and I can't wait to share it with them. It's the story about Ruth and Naomi, and I just adore the message.

I feel it's important for the children to understand the commitment to friendship and being loyal to one another. What I plan to teach them is that we can all gain God's grace through redemption and restoration. If we support one another, we can guide each other to the light and he will forgive. We just need to give it up to gain his love.

Feeling a little guilty at consuming too much of the hot water, I cut my shower short and step out. After toweling off, I wipe the mirror and stare at myself as I wet my toothbrush. Taking a deep breath, I can't help but notice the dark circles under my eyes. I'm not a particularly vain person, but I don't like the looks of it. I lied to my mother. I'm still not sleeping well and haven't for a while now. I toss and turn at night, thinking of Sam and how I'm allowing him to stray down the path, away from God. And I'm allowing him to do it by himself and that's just not right.

A knock at the door startles me. "Come on honey," my mother calls out. "I need in there."

"Sorry, just a moment," I reply as I wrap myself back in my towel and tuck my clothes under my arm.

After opening the door, I don't see her and assume she's returned to her bedroom. I quickly scurry to my room and close the door. We have two bathrooms in this house but the other is getting remodeled. It's an old house, and the drain began leaking from somewhere underneath and has made a mess of the ceiling downstairs. It's a pain sharing one bathroom, but it won't take the builders long to get us back to normal. At least, that's what my father says.

In the comfort of my bedroom, I notice the sun has recently risen and I open my curtains to allow the light to come in. The sun is already bright and illuminates the entire room. I drop my towel to the floor and dress quickly. My flowered shorts look cute and match my pink tank top perfectly. I'm thankful to work somewhere with a relaxed dress code. At least I'll be able to dress for the weather and not add to the heat with extra layers or the wrong material.

While sitting at my vanity, I apply a light coat of tinted moisturizer and basic eye shadow. I don't like to get carried away and my father hates I use any at all. After blow drying my hair, I lightly brush my blonde curls and hold them neatly together on top with a bow clip. Choosing sandals is easy with this sweltering heat. I pick the color closest to my bow and I'm happy to see they're lifted. At barely over five feet, I'll take any height advantage that I can get.

Feeling cute and happy to face the day, I straighten my bedroom and make my bed, as always. On my way down the stairs, my father calls out to me.

"No plans tomorrow," he states. "We're all going to hang around the house and get some work done. I'll grill something and we can make a day of it."

I nod and jog back up the stairs to kiss him on the cheek. "Yes, daddy," I say as I return to the stairs and head toward the door.

As I step outside, I instantly feel the heat. It's been hot lately, but this is different. I don't think it's supposed to be this hot, especially this early in the morning. I jog to my car, start the engine, and pull out of the drive, excited to see the children.

The drive to the daycare isn't far but I have time to think and I remember that my sister, Becca, wanted to help out today. I feel immediate regret for not asking my parents if it was OK once I approved it with the director. Oh well, I think. Maybe next time. I'd hate for my brother to be home all alone, anyway.

I turn my thoughts to Caden and can't wait to see him this afternoon. Lord, I love that boy. He's a little simple, but he loves me and he's up for whatever I want to do. When we were little, he used to protect me and make sure that I was involved in everything. I was always the leader of our group, but if something happened without me there, he made sure to tell me about it. He really is my one and only.

When we got old enough to know about dating, he asked me out and I said yes. We've been a couple ever since and we've never even thought about anyone else. I hope it remains that way for the rest of our lives. It would make me sick if I ever saw him with another girl and I'm not sure what I'd do. We're going to get married, right out of high school, and go off to college together. I know he's going to get a scholarship somewhere and I'll follow him. If it's too late for me to get a scholarship and my father won't pay for it, I'll do it myself. Anything, as long as I'm with him. He's my true companion.

While pulling into the parking spot, I second guess myself and pull out my phone to text Becca. Tyler will be home early, with football practice being held this morning, so he'll be able to tote my brother around. It'll be good for my sister to get out and have some responsibility. She's fourteen and needs to interact with others, and I think she'll love the children as much as I do.

"I forgot to ask dad if it's OK for you to help out at the daycare. If he says it is, you can walk up here and help today. Sorry."

I lay my phone in my purse before throwing it over my shoulder and stepping out of the car. It's definitely hot, and that sun is brutal. Maybe the Lord will bless us with a little bit of wind.

I'm early, but Miss Emily is already here and has the doors unlocked with all the lights on. I hear her in the back and announce myself, so as not to startle her. I'm relieved when she pokes her head around the corner and waves at me.

"Good morning," she calls out.

We each get to work, preparing for the day as we make small talk. I like Mrs. Emily. She's a gracious lady, probably in her early thirties, and does a good job of taking care of the children. Summer is busy at the daycare, because we have so many kids that are out of school and nowhere to go. They range, in age, from two to fifteen. I don't know why anyone wants to put their kid in daycare at fifteen. If they're not ready to take care of themselves by then, you've failed as a parent.

Mrs. Emily is from a few towns away and is accustomed to the small-town life. She married a guy that was born here, and they settled down, not far from the daycare. When Mrs. Liz retired, Emily took over. I think she's done a great job, and she's good with the kids. I just wish she was as smart as me. She could really make a difference with these children if she had my sensibility.

I feel a little guilty about leaving early today, but I always work late and ensure everything is well taken care of. I know Mrs. Emily is having her sister help this afternoon, and with my sister hopefully coming, surely, they can handle it by themselves. I'd hate for anything to happen to the children because I wasn't here. I don't know if I could come back from that. It would be awful and would devastate me.

The day runs smoothly. Becca shows up around ten, just in time for my bible story, and I think the kids enjoy it. I hope she takes something from it too. She needs more friends like I have. I spend a lot of time with Brooke's twin brothers. They crack me up, but they need a lot of attention. They see me often and enjoy my company. They're not bad kids, just rambunctious. I love them though and wouldn't want them any other way.

Mrs. Emily's sister comes in around eleven and helps me prepare lunch. It's nothing fancy, just peanut butter and jelly sandwiches with a fruit cup, but I enjoy getting to know her. She's only a few years younger than Mrs. Emily, but she looks much younger. I don't think she looks any older than my sister Becca. She's nice and good with the kids. When I go back to school, I think she should probably take over for me and work with her sister. If they can get along. I know siblings have a hard time working together, apart from my own, that is. My father taught us how and it's as easy as you make it. The trick is to accept one another's faults and pick up what they can't. Always support one another, plain and simple.

It's after one o'clock, and one child, young Abby, has breathing problems. It's nothing major, but her inhaler has run out and we don't have a spare. Mrs. Emily called her mother, who I've gotten to know well since I've been working here all summer, and she's on her way with another one. I like both the child and her mother. She's a strong woman and I admire her. Her name is Kelley Page, and she recently moved to town to be our police chief. That says something and sets a good example for young women everywhere. If you put your mind to it, you can do anything a man can do.

With everyone outside for playtime, I remain inside with Abby, keeping her company while we wait for her mom. I can tell she doesn't feel good and my heart breaks for her. I hate to see children get sick. I step to the window, and my eyes focus on Sammy when I recognize him immediately. He is leaning against the fence as Brooke's youngest brother, Jacob, offers to play catch. My stomach feels ill when. I see Mrs. Emily's sister jerk him away and stare at Sammy as if he is dirt. I notice the hurt in his eyes and feel the pain on his face. I feel it right along with him.

The broken man I see before me was once my best

friend. I miss Samantha with every ounce of my being and long to be with her again. It's as if she died and I grieve for her. We were inseparable. It was as common to see me with her as it was with my own siblings. She was family, and I loved her. I love her still.

My stomach churns as I watch him slink away. His head is down and he limps along the sidewalk. He appears as if he were a dog, kicked by his owner. A tear forms in my eye and my heart breaks. I retreat to the trash can and, without delay, throw up as I think of him. What a lonely world he lives in now. No one likes him and everyone abuses him. I grab a tissue and wipe my mouth as my sister and the child stare at me. I force a fake smile for them as I think of the horrible things that we've done to Sammy. Left all alone and forced to stand on the outside, looking in. Tears drip down my cheeks and I don't wipe them away. I deserve to feel this way. I deserve to hurt after what I've done. I swallow the vomit down my throat and stand tall, allowing myself to reflect on my behavior.

Samantha was a lovely girl. Caring, loving, and, most of all, supportive. She had the biggest heart of anyone I've ever known and only wanted the best for people. We grew up together and did everything as one person. Each of us intent on helping others and dreamed of a world with no hurt, abuse, or murder. We prayed together for others, even strangers. We fostered our friendships within the group and asked the Lord to protect them. We were companions. We were sisters.

I step back to the trash can and vomit a second time as I think about our meeting this afternoon. How hard it's going to be. How hard it's going to be to forgive. Will she forgive me? Will he forsake me? My heart is torn, but I know what I must do. I need to make it right. The Lord will never forgive me for my sins if I don't make this right. I will bring Samantha back and lead her to the promised land.

"Are you OK?"

I glance up to see Chief Kelley holding her daughter on her hip. Not knowing how long she's been standing there, I wipe the tears and my mouth. "I think so," I answer while forcing a smile. "Maybe the heat is getting to me."

"It'll do that to you," she acknowledges. "It's a hot one today."

I smile as I step forward and shake off my uneasy feeling. "Yes, it is."

The chief places her daughter on the counter and rifles through a paper bag that she brought with her. "How long has she been coughing and wheezing?" she asks.

I join them at the counter. "I noticed it right before Mrs. Emily called you." I answer. "And I've had her with me all morning, so I don't think it went unnoticed."

She smiles at me as she pulls an inhaler out of the bag and places the empty bag on the counter. "That's good. The faster we get her on the inhaler, the easier it is to deal with."

I nod in agreement as I watch her shake the inhaler before placing it to her daughter's lips. "Breathe deep, baby," she affectionately orders. She douses the inhaler while her daughter breathes in and I watch sympathetically as the poor child coughs deeply and pouts her lips. Tears form in the corners of her eyes and she appears miserable.

Chief Kelley rubs and caresses her head before kissing her on the forehead. When the coughing ceases, she offers it again. "One more time."

The child moans as she places her lips once more around the inhaler and receives a second dose. This time, the coughs are lighter, but she cries out as she coughs. Chief Kelley picks the little girl from the counter and wraps her in her arms while hugging her tightly and rubbing small circles on her back.

I feel the tenderness of a mother's love as I watch

the two of them. I cannot wait to have a child of my own and this is a perfect example of why. The joy and reward she must feel as she cares for her baby. It's something I long for and cannot wait to have Caden's child. We are going to be terrific parents.

Chief Kelley reaches the inhaler out to me behind her child's back. "Keep this one with you," she mutters. "I have another, and I trust you to administer it." She smiles at me. "Of course, always call me first. I don't trust anyone that much."

I chuckle aloud and understand what she means. "Thank you," I reply. "I understand."

She returns Abby to the counter and lifts her head as she kisses her on the forehead again. "Are you feeling better?" I watch sympathetically, as Abby nods her head, but still appears on the verge of tears. Her eyes are red around the edges and her lips are pouty. Bless her heart.

"Mommy has to go," she continues. "I love you and will be back to get you as soon as I can." She glances at me. "She'll be OK," she says. "She'll start feeling better in a little while and I'll come and get her as soon as I can."

I nod and attempt to make small talk. I like the chief and any opportunity I have to get her in my good graces is rewarding. "Busy day today."

She nods her head and opens a grin. "Busier than normal," she answers. "Jake Tuttle got drunk and shot and killed Mr. Smith's llama last night."

My mouth falls open. I love that llama and it's like Mr. Smith's baby. He's so proud of it. "Oh, no!" I exclaim. "Why would he do that?"

She chuckles a bit. "It's not funny," she states as she attempts not to laugh. "But he thought it was a deer." She shakes her head. "He already admitted to it and feels real bad. Especially this morning."

Shocked by the news, I don't think it's funny at all

and don't smile. How can a person be so careless like that? So I want our group to slow down our drinking. Something bad is bound to happen and I wouldn't like that very much. "What's going to happen to him?" I ask and hope he gets in big trouble.

She shrugs her shoulders. "Don't know. He also punched Deputy Paul, so he's facing assault charges. I can only gather the evidence. It'll be up to the judge and jury." She shakes her head again. "I feel bad for all of them."

I put on a sad face, but I don't actually feel bad for Jake, only Mr. Smith and Paul. "I'll pray for them," I announce.

She smiles at me. "That's real nice," she replies before turning to hug and kiss her child again. "Mommy has to go. I love you."

Abby whimpers as she grips on to Kelley's neck. I step forward and gently pick the little girl up and pull her hands from around her mother's neck as I wrap her in my arms. Her head falls against my neck and I hug her affectionately.

While smiling kindly at me, Chief Kelley rubs her daughter's back and places her hand on my arm. "Thank you," she mutters. "Thank you for being so kind to my girl."

"Of course," I reply.

"I mean it," she says. "You're a good person and it makes me happy to know that my child will be cared for while she's here."

My heart feels full upon hearing her words, and I feel myself blush. Her phone rings from her pocket and I watch as she answers it. Her face drops, and she turns away from me.

"Dammit," she calls out. "I was just right there. I was at the pharmacy." She glances back at me briefly before staring at the floor. "Is he on the way to the hospital?" She pauses and I assume someone is answering her on the other end. "Is he going to be OK?"

Her troubled face worries me; I fear something bad has happened. I try to listen to the conversation, but I can only hear a murmur through the speaker.

"Well, that's good, I guess," she says with a sigh. "I'll be right there." She slides the phone back in her pocket and turns to me. "Gotta go. Call me if you need me."

Before I can say another word to her, she turns and exits the room. With the child held securely in my arms, I dance softly toward the window and begin humming a gospel tune as I rub at her back. While looking out over the children as they're busy at play, I can't help but feel satisfied and full of love for each of them.

I bow my head and speak a prayer for Mr. Smith and his pet llama. I pray he will find peace and forgiveness in his heart. I pray the Lord rewards him and blesses him as he sees fit. I turn my prayer to Jake Tuttle. I pray he finds the punishment he deserves and that the punishment brings him closer to God. I pray Jake finds redemption once the Lord has issued his retribution. At the end, I call for God to watch over Chief Kelley and the people involved in whatever she just discussed on the phone. I hope everyone is alright.

Thinking of the prayer I bestowed on Jake, turns my focus once again to Sammy. I feel my stomach churn at the thought of this afternoon's meeting and dread the outcome. I know we must do it and hopefully bring him closer to the Lord. We will mend our friendship and we will make this right. I place the child to the floor as I once again retreat to the trash can and vomit into it.

Feeling downright ill, I know I need to go home and rest before we meet him this afternoon. I'll pray on it, and hopefully the Lord will repair my sickness so I can bring Samantha back to us. He'll give me the strength I need to get through the hardships we will all face.

I hear the door close as my father walks across the

floor, sorting mail. I sit up as he walks next to me and takes a seat in his recliner.

"Hey pumpkin, you awake?"

I smile and nod at him. "Yeah," I answer. "That nap felt good." I've actually been awake for a little while. I've just been laying here. Caden texted me about Brock getting in a fight, and I couldn't go back to sleep after that. I hope Brock is OK.

He laughs as he powers the television on. "Just saw Sam. She needs to stay off my grass."

I smile, although the thought of him makes my stomach hurt again. I need to get around and get this over with. Following a quick nap, I still don't feel quite right. My stomach hurts and I feel sad. After rising from the couch, I notice the time and decide to text Caden back.

"Are you there yet? How's Sam acting?" I ask.

"Not ther yet. Drivin around for a minute. Ready to get this over wit so we can party."

"OK." I respond before laying my phone on the coffee table. I really need to turn on this boy's auto-correct. I stand to my feet and lift my hands over my head as I stretch them as far as I can reach. It feels good to hear my bones pop. My phone dings again.

"How you feeling?"

I sigh, knowing I need to end this message and get moving. I can probably still catch them, if I hurry. *"Better. See you there."*

"Good deal. Love you."

I drop my phone and rush upstairs. I hurriedly fix my hair and splash water across my face. I jog to my bedroom and put on my shoes. I need to hurry. I'll just come back here after we meet with Sam to get my stuff for tonight.

After kissing my father on the cheek, I grab my phone and rush to the door. "I'm going for a walk," I call out.

"OK," he laughs. "But it's too hot to be out walking

around."

Without responding, I close the door and walk briskly down the sidewalk. Just a short distance down the road, I spot Caden's Jeep and pull out my phone.

"I'm coming now. I'm feeling better and I see you. Wait there for me."

I see them exit the Jeep and watch as they circle up. I pick up my pace. I don't like the idea of anyone waiting for me. Especially Sam. I know he'll be nervous and I don't want to draw this out.

"Hey babe," Caden says as he reaches out to embrace me. "You feeling better?"

I nod, although my stomach is in butterflies. I dread this and the anticipation is killing me. "I am."

"You OK, Ally?" Brooke asks and actually appears concerned. "We don't have to do this today if you're not feeling well."

I shake my head. "No," I answer sternly. "Today is the day. We need to make this right."

"And what is it you hope to accomplish?" Millie asks. "You think everything is going to go back to the way it used to be?"

"This is bullshit," adds Brock. "I shouldn't be here."

I take a deep breath and strengthen myself. "Enough," I bark. "We're doing this whether you like it or not." I take a moment to look each of them in the eye. "If you don't want to be here, then go." I again glance from one to the other. "But you better not say anything. We take care of each other in this group. We're a family."

Everyone falls silent, and they turn their heads to the ground. "Good," I continue. "Let's get this over with so we can all move on."

I turn and begin across the park, not looking back to see if the others follow.

"Look babe," Caden calls out. "I think Sam puked

from the heat. Millie said he got fat!"

Brock Williams

It's a quarter after six and I know I need to hurry. Caden will be here soon, to pick me up, but I must take care of the rabbits. I mowed over their den and killed most of them, including the mother, but there's two babies in the shed out back that I'm trying to nurse and I hope to save their lives.

It's dark, and this flashlight needs a charge. As I open the door, I see the glow from the heat lamp and step in its direction. My shin strikes an old bar bell and I cry out in agony. I know I need to remain quiet, but my anger causes me to kick the bar, and it rolls across the floor, nearly knocking the tank off the counter. Quickly, I jump forward and grab onto it before steadying the supports underneath of the makeshift counter. That could've been bad. I'm keeping them in an old fish tank and the glass would've shattered and probably killed them, even if the fall didn't.

I breathe heavily out of my mouth and try to relax my anger away, just as the psychologist advised. I've been so mad lately and I can't seem to get it under control. I don't want to talk to my school counselor about it. He's liable to put me back into therapy again. It's not fun to sit and talk to someone when all they do is judge you.

I take my time to feed the bunnies, holding them close as they suckle at the bottle. They're so cute and make me feel good about caring for them. I enjoy feeding them. It makes me feel like I have purpose and there's not a lot of that in my life. I hate I will not get to do it anymore today, since I have to work and I have Caden's party tonight. I should probably skip it, but I rarely have any fun. Nah, I need to go. It'll make me feel better and I'll just have my little brother, Blake, care for them while I'm gone. He'll enjoy being in charge and he's been doing a good job of caring for them, too. Neither of us has much in our lives, so taking care of the bunnies is a big deal for the two of us.

After laying the bunnies back in the tank, I take another minute to rub them before carefully crossing the floor and exiting the shed. As I climb the steps to the house, I notice the handrail is wobbly and will need repaired. I'll add it to my already long list of things to do. I open the screen door and pin it behind my back as I attempt to gently open the door. It's old and doesn't sit in the frame quite right, so I have to force it and flinch when I hear it groan loudly as it bursts open.

While stepping inside, and already feeling ashamed that I made such a loud noise with the door, I step lightly as the floor creaks under foot. I don't want to wake the others in the house. My brother needs all the rest he can get, and I really don't want to hear my mom's mouth this morning. She's angry all the time, and she's been on me to earn more money with the high electric bill. She runs the air conditioner on full blast and this shitty house isn't insulated very well, so it's always hot. I'll save no money if she keeps running through it. I do my best, though. With my father gone, I need to help where I can. Even if she doesn't appreciate it.

I rifle through the cabinets, searching for something to eat but come up empty. I thought she had just gone grocery shopping. The food stamps hit earlier this week and I pray she didn't sell them again. I step to the refrigerator and first look in the freezer. Nothing but ice cube trays. When I open the refrigerator, I smell a foul odor and quickly determine it is leftover cabbage that was left uncovered. While scanning around, I notice there's nothing in here outside of condiments. I grab the cabbage and toss it in the garbage before closing the door. Disappointed, I know I'll need to have a tough conversation with her when I come home. In the meantime, I'll just have Blake meet me at the diner for lunch. That way, I won't have to worry about him going hungry.

As I tie up the garbage bag, I hear Caden honk his horn out front. Damn him, I think. Quickly, I pull the garbage bag out of the can and pick up my change of clothes for tonight. After stuffing them under my arm, I dart out the door and turn up the side of the house. I take only a moment to throw the garbage in the bin before Caden honks again.

I rush to the front of the house and jerk the door of his Jeep open. "What the hell, man?" I call out. "Don't wake my family up."

The music is blaring, and as he reaches up to turn it down, he glances at me blankly. "What?"

I shake my head and climb into the seat. Before I even settle in, he reverses out of the driveway and lurches forward as he speeds down the street.

"I brought you an Uncrustable," he says as he reaches it out to me.

Happy to have it, I take it from his hand and open the package. "Thanks man," I reply. "I'm starving and there's nothing in there to eat."

He shakes his head and bites his lower lip. "You want me to stop at the store?"

"Nah," I answer. "I don't have the money to spend. I'll just wait until lunch."

He nods as he pushes on the throttle and cranks the music, singing at the top of his lungs. I watch as he plays the air guitar, and he continually glances in my direction since I'm his only fan. Caden is a terrible singer and sings mostly off rhythm, but he is entertaining. The kid doesn't care what anyone thinks of him and he knows I have his back, no matter what.

He's my best friend and like my brother. We've been around each other for our entire lives and he's done so much for me. If it wasn't for fear of leaving my brother Blake alone at home, I'd have left a long time ago to move in with him and his family. They wouldn't mind. They love me. I'm like another kid to them and they watch out for me. Most people don't know it, but they've bought me school clothes and fed me whenever I need it. They have said nothing to me and I don't think they've ever bragged about it to anyone else. They're just good people and I love them dearly.

With Caden's dad getting sick, it's been a little weird around there. Everyone is so sad. I like to go visit with him and do things around the house because Caden will not do it. His dad has been like a father to me, and I'll miss him when he dies. I'm pretty sure he got me the job at the mill, and I'm forever grateful for it. It's him or grandpa but it doesn't matter. I'll do anything for anyone in his family.

Caden and I have always pushed each other and I think that's why we're such excellent athletes. He's taller than me, but at six foot two, I'm not small. I'm definitely faster and stronger than him, but not by much. I have him edged out because I've had to work my entire life and I have the strength that comes from somewhere deep within. Caden got his athletic prowess through genetics. Both his grandpa and his dad were top-notch athletes, and he's no exception. Although, he's lazy, mostly, he works very hard on the football field and there hasn't been an arm talent like his around these parts in forever. He's on a different level.

Other than our athletic ability, that's the only thing we have in common and I don't know how we're such good friends. Our physical appearance is completely different. He's light headed, I'm dark. He has blue eyes; I have brown. He's skinny, and I'm thicker. He's good looking and I'm average, at best. Our personalities are polar opposites. He's funny, charming, and outgoing. Whereas I'm angry, sad, and hate everyone outside of my family and four friends. I guess we're like salt and pepper. We just go together.

He screeches to a stop in the parking lot, and my body lurches forward into the dashboard. I turn to glare at him and notice that he's all smiles.

"Just wakin' you up, bro," he boasts. "Looked like you were asleep over there."

I grit my teeth and shake my head. "I'm gonna kick your ass today," I mutter.

"Easy, killer," he jokes. "Let's get through practice first."

I step out as he joins me on the passenger side. "Can you drop me at work when practice is over?" I ask.

"For sure."

"Thanks," I reply as I stuff my change of clothes under the seat. "Then I'm just gonna leave my clothes in the Jeep."

"Bro, you gotta get a bag."

I smile as we walk toward the field. "Had one. Don't know where it's at."

I notice the stadium lights are already on as we cut through the tunnel into the locker room. As we get dressed, boys keep shuffling in and joke with each other as we suit up. I stay to myself and focus on getting dressed quickly. I'm a little sore from work yesterday and want to get in some extra stretches to get loosened up. I've never bagged so many pounds of feed in my life. One boy called out and left me by myself, but I got the job done and I think my boss was happy.

When we finish stretching and run our laps, we get right to it. Our first game of the season is right around the corner and we don't have any time to spare. This is our year to win state and we will let nothing stop us. We will be prepared.

For most of the practice, we line up with starting offense against starting defense. We rotate players in and out, but, as the stars, Caden and I are in on almost every play. We're shredding them too. That poor defense can't keep up. We're running all over the place and throwing the ball at will. Near the end of the practice, another senior, that plays defensive line, gets mad and hits Caden a little harder than I like. He's a big boy and when Caden flies backward, he hits the ground hard and I hear him cry out in pain. The anger flashes over me and I attack. I hit him on his blind side and drive him to the ground. When I roll him to his back, I can see the pain in his eyes as I lift his helmet and punch him in the mouth.

"You do that again!" I yell out. "And I'll kill you."

He lifts his hands to his face as I rare back to hit him again. I feel multiple sets of hands wrap around my arm and lift me from his body. As they pull me backward, I shake free and leap back on top of the boy, swinging wildly at his face but mostly hitting his helmet. I hear the coach screaming in the background as the guys once again pull me off. He crawls away, and I want nothing more than to go back at him. Just as I begin to, once again, pull away, the coach grabs me by the face mask.

"Williams!" he screams. "You're done. Hit the showers!"

Hesitantly, I march across the field toward the locker room. I hear the coach shout out behind me.

"I want you both in my office after practice."

I keep my head down and know that I won't be there. What's he going to do? He can't bench me, I'm too good. If I go in there and see that guy right now, it won't be good.

I'm in Caden's Jeep, with the seat laid back when he finally comes out. He looks surprised but only laughs as he climbs in and passes me a sandwich out of a vending machine.

"Coach is looking for you," he laughs. "He's pretty mad."

I tear open the sandwich and take a bite. "Thanks," I say. "He'll get over it." I turn to look at him as he backs out of the parking lot. "Where did you get this? There's not any vending machines in there."

He puts the car in gear and winks at me as he takes off. "Coach's desk."

We both get a laugh as he speeds away and cranks the music. Caden loves to listen to music and always at high volume.

It's not far from the football field to the mill, and as Caden pulls up, I notice his face is somber. He turns the volume down before turning to face me.

"Bro, you can't do that," he mutters. "You don't have to protect me. I can take care of myself."

"I know," I respond. "I just got mad."

He shakes his head and sighs aloud. "I know, but I don't want you to have to go back to therapy. You gotta control your anger."

"I know," I repeat as I sigh aloud. I know he's right and I don't know why I've been so mad lately. I need to cut it out, though. I just don't know how. It feels like I'm going to explode. "I'm sorry, bro."

"No problem, man. I'm just worried about you."

We slap a handshake and say our goodbyes as I grab my change of clothes and climb out of the Jeep to walk toward the mill. I really don't want to work today and wish I could go to the creek with him to get the party ready, but I need the money. I dread this heat today and they say it's going to be boiling.

The morning at the mill runs easy. The other guy, Rob, is back, and he said that he's sorry he caused me so much work yesterday. I told him I'd forgive him if he took me to lunch at the diner and he agreed. I text my brother and he's going to meet us there. I feel a little proud that I was able to get a free meal out of the guy. I was just doing my job, but I'll take it. It's hot work today and I feel like my knees are going to give out, but we make it through. I think I've drunk ten gallons of water from the fountain and can't seem to quench my thirst. I bet it's not this hot in the Sahara Desert.

At the last minute, and right before we prepare to go to lunch, an order comes in and we need to fill it before we're able to leave. The order is complicated and time consuming. I hate the idea that Blake will be waiting for us, and I'm seriously hungry. I don't like late lunches. My stomach knows when lunch is supposed to be and I like to eat at noon, no matter what.

I feel pangs of hunger running through my stomach as we step into the diner, and I'm surprised to see so many people still here. I didn't know this many people took late lunches. We spot my brother Blake in the back while he vigorously waves us over. The place is crowded and our table is in the very back of the diner, tucked in a corner. We take a seat and the server approaches our table almost instantly.

Sticking with my go to, I order a bacon cheeseburger, large fry, and a Coke. This place has the best cheeseburgers and there's no need for me to try something different. They both order the same as I did and we begin conversation.

Blake is not like me. He's outgoing and able to speak with other people without worry of being judged. The two of them hit it off and find they have a common interest. My brother is an outdoorsman and loves to fish. That's how he spends most of his day and the two of them can't stop talking about it. I sit quietly as they tell each other stories and talk about the excellent fishing spots they know. I'm not a big fisherman. Caden likes it and I go with him sometimes, but it's not really for me.

Usually, when Caden goes fishing, he takes Ally and I hang out with Brooke or Millie. Millie's easier for me to hang with because she's so outgoing and carries most of the conversation. She's gotten me to try more stuff than all the others combined, and I love her for it. She's such a wild soul. Brooke is just Brooke. She's my friend and I love her, but we have a hard time finding things to do when it's just the two of us. She's always so serious and I really don't like to talk. I love her soul and she's so caring that it's hard for me not to love her. It's best when we all hang out together as a group. It just works well with all of our different personalities.

Since Caden and I are such good buddies, I hang out with him and Ally all the time. I'm their third wheel, but they don't seem to mind. Ally's a pretty serious person, but she knows how to have a good time and how to help me have a good time. I know she prays for me a lot because she tells me so. I love Ally as much as I love Caden and it's nice to have such good friends. I'm always so lonely when I'm at home, and having them around gives me hope in this world.

When the food arrives, the conversation falls and is almost nonexistent while we eat. I eat fast and slide my basket forward when I finish. As they eat, I sip on the Coke and wait patiently for them to finish.

"Ain't that your girlfriend?"

I glance up to see that Rob is nodding toward the door, so I turn in my seat to take a look. Not knowing what to expect, I'm surprised to see Sam standing at the counter, looking around. I slump down, not wanting him to see me. I can't believe he's here and I can't believe he called him my girlfriend.

Rob notices how I squirm in my seat and how I work to keep low, out of eyesight. I hear him laugh. "What are you doing?" he asks.

I shake my head and feel the heat rise in my ears. "Nothing," I answer. "I don't want to see him."

Rob, thinking it's a joke, waves his hand in the air while grinning from ear to ear. "Over here," he calls out. "Your boyfriend is over here."

Anger flashes through me, and I grab his arm, pulling it down. "Don't do that," I growl.

Rob appears unfazed and laughs even louder. He thinks he's onto a good joke, but he doesn't understand. He lifts his other hand and I squeeze hard on his wrist, turning it inward and applying pressure. I can feel it about to snap as my outrage boils over.

"Hey man!" he cries out. "You're hurting me!"

I feel the temperature rise along my face. I'm hot and it isn't from the weather. I glare at him as Blake reaches for my arm. My head snaps toward my brother and I see the concern on his face.

"Relax Brock," he whispers. "Let him go."

Seeing my brother's face eases my tension and I release him. Glancing around, I see a few people looking at us, and they appear to be worried. I feel uneasy and embarrassed as I glance back toward Sam to see him holding a stack of shirts. Rob pushes his trash forward.

"It's time to go," he grumbles. "I'm getting out of here."

He stands to his feet, and I immediately bark at him. "Sit back down!"

"No way," he returns. "You're nuts."

He walks toward the counter, and I follow him with my eyes. As he approaches, I watch as Sam turns and exits the door. I feel the anger boiling within me as I watch him leave. I remain seated and feel the fury rise inside, even as Blake speaks to me. I don't know what he says. I feel blank and my mind races. I can't focus on anything. I want blood.

After Rob pays and steps out the door, I rise from my seat and make a beeline for the exit. As I step out on the sidewalk, I see Sam step into the pharmacy and immediately turn toward the alley, and therefore, the parking lot. Blake is right on my heels and he yells at me, but I still don't understand his words.

Leaning against his car, Rob lights a cigarette as I approach. "Hey man," he calls out. "I don't know what your problem is, but I was only joking."

Rage bursts from my soul, and I yell at him. "You think it's a joke! I'll show you a joke!"

He never lifts his hands. It's as if he thinks less of me, and while he inhales from his cigarette, my first punch hits him in the mouth. I rage at him, cussing and screaming as his body crumples to the ground. Fury consumes my entire core as I climb on top of him and swing wildly. His body goes stiff, and while I strike at his face, he slides underneath his pickup truck. I'm overwhelmed with outrage and I inflict a devastating amount of damage as I unleash my wrath. Blood pours from his nose and mists in the air as I land shot after shot to his head.

I hear Blake yelling, and feel him on my back, but he's only a gnat to me and I swat him away. My anger overwhelms my sensibility, and I feel nothing but rage. My eyes watch as I brutalize Rob and I'm unable to stop myself.

When the first blow hits my head, I feel only the

recoil of my neck. When the second is delivered, I stop and turn to see Blake standing over me, prepared to swing again. He is crying and begging me to stop. I turn back to Rob. His face is purple and bloody. His body convulses wildly and I stand to my feet. Still feeling nothing for Rob, I feel the energy dissipate from my body and my hands relax. Fear takes over and I nervously peer around. Nobody has shown up, but I'm sure they will.

"I have to get out of here," I call out to Blake. "Where's your bike?"

While he cries, he points toward the back door of the diner and I take off, yelling to him as I pass. "I'll call you when I get somewhere to hide."

He mutters something, but not loud enough for me to hear as I leap on his bike and pedal away. I cut down side streets and pedal as if my life depends on it. I keep from the sidewalk, sticking to the road as I navigate around the few cars that pass. With my legs churning, I carry myself through the neighborhood and reach a large field. The hay is thick and slows the bike as I work to push through. Hesitantly, I leap from the bike and toss it to the ground as I take off on foot. My heart is pounding and I'm running short of breath, but I push forward and continue. I see woods ahead and know that will lend me concealment.

Just a few feet into the woods, I slow my jog and eventually come to a stop as I double over. I can't breathe and my lungs burn as I search around, trying to recognize my location. Just ahead, and less than twenty yards away, I spot the creek and feel that I know where I am. I take off again toward the creek, cutting through the timber and wiggling through briars. As I reach the creek, nearing exhaustion, and burning up from the heat, I collapse at its water's edge. I pull my shirt from my body and reach into the water, splashing it across my face and along my torso. I need to cool myself. While glancing down, I see the pink water running along my forearm and turn my hand over. My knuckles are shredded and blood covers my hand. I wash it quickly, but realize I probably have it all over my face. I pick my shirt up and dunk it under the water. Vigorously, I scrub at my face and chest as I blindly clean myself.

I reach in my pocket for my phone but come up empty. I search through all of my pockets but can't find it anywhere. Panic strikes me and I fear I left it on the table at the diner. Oh well, I think. There's nothing I can do about it now.

My breathing reduces and I glance up. Figuring that I need to get out of here, I know where I must go. I wrap the shirt around my hand and continue north along the creek. Caden's grandfather's cabin is just a few miles ahead. He'll take care of me until we can figure this out.

I jog along the creek bank, darting into the thicket when I can't find a trail. Fear overwhelms me now and I worry about Rob. I never intended to hurt him. I just couldn't stop myself. I feel like I'm about to tear up and I never cry. I like the guy and truly regret doing that to him. I can't believe I let my anger get away from me. They told me last time that I was in big trouble if it ever happens again. Now look at me. I've done it and I fear I've hurt him worse than I can handle. I don't want to hurt anyone. It just comes out of me.

As I run along, I feel the heat bearing down on me and it's overwhelming. I'm thankful to be in good shape and thankful I've been working in the hot mill. I don't think I could handle this jog if it weren't for my conditioning. I really hope Caden is at the cabin. I know he's preparing for a party, but I'm not sure if he's still there. He may have gone to care for his father and I worry I will miss him. I breathe through my nose as I trudge along. Oh well, I think. He'll come back and I can wait for him there. They never lock the cabin and they won't mind. They will protect me.

I think about missing our meeting with Sam and I feel instant regret. Although I won't admit it to anyone, I wanted to hear from him. I wanted to see what he has to say, and I wanted to see if my Samantha was in there somewhere. I know Ally said she can bring Samantha back, but I don't know how. I fear Samantha is gone forever. She's only a fleeting memory and I think we're supposed to view her as something from the past and accept her for what she is now. I miss her. I long to see her and talk to her. Why can't she just come back? I love her.

I have a strong relationship with each of the others in the group, and Caden is definitely my best friend. However, I loved Samantha more than any of them. I wanted her to be my girlfriend, and I wanted us to be together. I can't believe this happened and I still can't believe her choice in changing.

We were always the most alike one another and I'm not sure she realized how close we truly were. I never told her how I felt because I assumed she knew. We shared something special. We were each abused by our fathers and both raised poor. None of the others understands what that does to you. We did, though. We knew. I was always in awe at how she could find love in others, even after what her father did to her, and again when she became Sam. They are each so forgiving and caring of the people around them; even those who've done them wrong. I've often thought about her face, from when we were younger, and how she looked at the world. She was so lovely and cared for everyone and everything. I wanted that, and I wanted someone in my life that could bring that to me.

My chest burns as I gulp at air and push forward. It's so hot and I can barely think as I run to my hideaway.

I've observed Sam as people bully him and see resemblances of Samantha. He looks so hurt when people abuse him and he always approaches them as if he has forgiven them. I often wonder if he's the same person I fell in love with and, just as often, regret not confessing my love to Samantha. I have secretly looked forward to this meeting and desire nothing more than to understand. I miss my Samantha so much and don't understand how she can disappear from my life. I should have told her. I should have told her how I felt. I now long to hear from the person she has become to find out where she's gone. I need to know what Sam has done with her or if she's still in there somewhere.

I burst through the opening to the gravel bar and watch as Caden climbs in his Jeep. I call out, but my voice doesn't work. I swallow what moisture remains in my mouth and call out again. Nothing. While mustering everything I have left, I call out.

"Caden!" I scream. "Don't leave me!"

Police Chief Kelley Page

"Do we know who did this?" I ask as I approach the crime scene.

Leaned over the hood of the victim's truck is Deputy Carl smoking a cigarette and sweating profusely. He's chatting with the manager of the diner, who I've met a few times and seems to be OK. I think his name is Tom, but I'm not completely positive.

"We're pretty sure that it's the older Williams boy," he answers after turning and flicking his cigarette into the street.

I turn to watch his cigarette fly through the air and bounce across the pavement a few times before rolling to the curb. I hate cigarettes, but I hate smokers even more when think they can litter their butts all over the place. I turn back toward Deputy Carl and notice he stands in blood as he chats with the manager.

"Carl!" I call out while pointing toward his feet. "You're standing in the evidence."

Carl glances down and lifts each of his feet as he peers at the soles of his shoes. His gigantic body struggles to lift his legs, and he scrunches his nose. "Gross!" He exclaims as he shuffles to the front of the vehicle. "It's not much for evidence."

I shake my head and pull out my notepad. "Who is the victim?"

He turns to face me but rests his butt against the grill of the pickup. "Rob Stewart," he answers. "Twenty-seven. White male."

"Have you notified his loved ones?"

Carl wipes the sweat from his forehead with the back of his hand. Sweat accumulates around the collar of his shirt and I'm almost positive that I can smell him from here. "Doesn't have any," he answers. "Moved to town a few years back when he was dating the Medlin girl. They split up, and he stayed around. Had to arrest him this winter for stalking her." He smiles, although I don't find it funny. "Guess he still wants her."

I nod. "I'm sure he has family. Start with the Medlin girl and see if she has any contacts. We need to notify the family." He nods as I continue. "Now tell me about the suspect."

I take notes as Carl gives me the backstory on Brock Williams. It sounds like he's had a tough life and I feel like he's definitely the prime suspect. Especially when Carl tells me about his past assault cases and how the judge ordered him to undergo therapy. That was nice of the judge and probably saved him from spending a little time in jail. I don't think it's going to save him this time, though. I need to find out what shape the victim is in.

"He's a football star," Carl states proudly after finishing up. "Should help us get to state this year."

Great, I think to myself. A football star in a small town. What could go wrong with that? "And what leads you to believe he's the guilty party?"

Carl speaks, but the manager of the diner interrupts. "People inside saw him grabbing Rob's arm," he says. "They said he looked furious, and they were having somewhat of an argument."

I glance at Carl. "Did you get their statement?"

Carl puts his head down and appears embarrassed. "No. I forgot."

I shake my head and glance back at the manager. "Anything else?"

"They work at the feed mill together. I went in there to get a bag of dog food last week and they were both working the warehouse." The manager sighs aloud. "He's a pretty good kid," he continues. "Guess he just got mad."

I nod, even though I don't care for his opinion on the matter. "Anything else that I need to know?"

"Just one more thing," he answers. "The boy left his phone on the table when he split. Looks like he was in a hurry to get out of here and forgot it."

"Who?" I ask. "The suspect? Brock?"

The manager nods his head as Carl fishes around in his pocket before pulling out a phone and offers it to me. I stare at him blankly. Did he really just have the suspect's phone in his pocket and now handles it without gloves?

"Carl," I speak directly. "Set it on the hood. You're supposed to wear gloves and catalog all evidence. That's how we're going to tie him to this location."

Carl places the phone on the hood and shuffles his feet. It appears as if he doesn't know what to do or where to go. I shake my head and walk to my cruiser before returning with an evidence bag and a pair of gloves.

As I put on the gloves, I glance at Carl. "Get this man's statement." I glance up at the manager. "What was your name, sir?"

"Tom," he states proudly. "Tom Jackson."

I smile, feeling proud that I remembered his name. I turn back to Carl as I slide the phone into the bag and seal it. "When you're done with him, get statements from the other witnesses." I make eye contact. "Do you remember who they are?"

Carl nods and appears sheepish. "Yes, I do."

"Good," I continue. "I'm going by the feed mill and the Williams residence before I drive to the hospital. Call me if you need me." I turn toward my cruiser before second guessing myself. "Carl," I call out. "Photograph the scene with measurements. Collect samples of the blood and get multiples." I step forward. "Might have the suspect's blood in there as well." I double down, even though I don't want to make him feel stupid. "You know how to do that, right?"

Carl nods again and repeats himself. "Yes, I do."

"OK," I say. "Call me when you're done, so I can let you know where I am. That is, if I don't call you first." I nod my head at him. "Call me before you leave the crime scene. I may want additional evidence collected, but let me think on it."

I doubt I will, but I don't want to put him on the spot for not trusting in him to do his job correctly. I turn toward my cruiser and walk halfway before turning back around. He still rests on the bumper of the victim's pickup and has resumed his conversation with Tom.

"Carl," I call out. "One more thing."

I see Carl sigh and I feel like he expects me to give him more orders. "You can change into a tee shirt today. It's too hot to wear the entire uniform." I smile at him when I see him smile. "Get comfortable buddy. It may be a late night."

It makes me happy that I'm able to end my encounter with Carl on a positive note. However, I don't just do it for him to be comfortable. He's very overweight, and I'd hate to lose him to a heat stroke or heart attack while he stands in this heat. Carl is a nice guy and I get tired of being on him for poor police work. He's a slob, and lazy, and when you mix that with low intelligence, you have a recipe for disaster. What am I going to do, though? It's not like people are lined up around the block to come and work here for fourteen dollars an hour.

I climb into my cruiser and feel thankful that I left it running. The air is cold and feels fantastic. I lay the suspect's phone in the passenger seat and take a drink from my water bottle. As I turn out of the parking lot, I radio to dispatch. "Tina," I say. "Do you have a copy?" I wait a moment before repeating myself with a slightly elevated tone. "Tina. Do you have a copy?"

"I'm here, chief," she answers. "What's up?"

I shake my head at the lack of professionalism in this department. I've been in this town for two months, and even I have relaxed on using proper codes and lingo when on the radio. It's not just that, this is a good ole boy community, and nothing like the big city. The mayor, the judge, all the city council members; they're all simple, down-to-earth people, and don't do anything like where I come from.

"I need everything you have on Brock Williams and everything you have on Rob Stewart. Both with standard spelling, I believe."

She is silent for a moment. "Football Brock?" she questions.

I sigh aloud. "Yes, football Brock."

"He's the one that beat up that guy?" she asks.

"Possibly," I return and lose my patience. "Looking into him, and I need his files."

"What a shame," she admits. "He's probably going to lead us to state." I remain silent as she continues. "OK chief. I'll get both of them to you as soon as I can. You want me to send it to your cruiser?"

"That would be great," I answer. "I'll be out searching for him."

"OK chief. You might check with Caden Astor. Those two are thick as thieves. They play football with my boy and they're always around one another. You want me to send his info, too?"

"Yes please," I answer, and a little proud of her for going the extra mile. "And Tina. Call the hospital and check on the victim for me. I'm headed that way soon and would like to know how he's doing."

"Will do, chief," she responds. "Should have all the files on your computer in fifteen minutes."

In the two months since I've been the Police Chief in this town, I haven't seen a lot of action. I came here from a big city, up north, where I worked as a deputy. We'd see this kind of stuff multiple time a day, and so much worse. It was terrible with all the crime and I hate how bad people treat one another in this world. I just don't get it. It's been nice in this town, and feels like a community where people look after one another. Outside of Jake shooting Mr. Smith's llama, I have had little to do. Just the occasional DUI or domestic dispute, but most of those get resolved pretty easily.

I took this job, and brought my daughter down here, after my husband took off with another woman and left me in pieces. He never even cared when I told him I was taking our daughter, three states away. What a piece of shit! It's been nice starting over and I like this community. Sure, I miss the big city, but this place grows on me, more and more, every day.

The drive to the feed mill isn't far, and when I climb

back out into the heat, I instantly feel the skin on my face warm under the intense sunrays glaring down from overhead. I'll need to put on some sunscreen if I plan to be out in this for very long. My milky complexion burns easily and I don't want peeling skin on my nose without having been to a beach to earn it. It's not right to get a sunburn when you're only climbing in and out of a cruiser. My blonde hair gets lighter from the sun and it has been brutal the last few weeks. I worry it's going to make me look like I bleach it and don't want folks talking. I'm not overly superficial, but I like to look nice. I'm tall and slender, with an athletic build. Since coming to this town, I've had a lot of time for the gym, and at thirty years old, I'm in the best shape of my life. My face is cute enough. I moisturize and have excellent complexion, so that helps. I have bright blue eyes and a small nose over thin lips. I've had cosmetologists show me how to apply lipstick to make my lips appear fuller, but I choose to go natural. Sure, I'll use a little foundation, but I don't get carried away. My heart is still broken and I'm not looking for love. Not right now, anyway.

I walk inside, and it takes only a minute to locate the manager. He's actually the owner, and based on his appearance, he should've retired ten years ago. He's sharp as a tack, though, and when I tell him what happened, I'm shocked at the sheer volume of curse words he has in his vocabulary. I've never, in my life, heard an old man talk this way. He's furious at the both of them and holds Rob, just as accountable as he holds Brock. He doesn't care why it happened. He has orders to fill and nobody left to fill them. Other than his anger, he doesn't offer much information that I don't already know. He tells me he gave the job to Brock as a favor to Caden's grandpa and that, overall, he's a good kid and a hard worker. He tells me that the two had no problems working together and he's surprised to hear what happened now. I leave him my card and ask him to call me if he hears from Brock. Although, I fear he will just put him back to work and won't bother calling.

Just as I slide in my cruiser and close the door, I glance at the screen of my computer and see that Tina sent me the files I had requested. When I click on one to open, my radio sounds out. "Chief, do you have a copy?"

"Go ahead, Carl," I answer.

"Looks like Blake, the younger brother, was with them at the diner."

"Who's younger brother?" I ask. "Brock?"

"That's right," he returns. "Brock's younger brother, Blake, was having lunch with them. I got it from one of the witnesses. Blake is probably fourteen or fifteen years old."

"Good work, Carl," I assert.

"Thanks," he cheerily responds, and I imagine his smiling face and picture him happy from my words of praise.

See, I think to myself. This is why we take statements and talk to witnesses. Maybe I'll bring it up to him later, as a teachable moment.

I pull up the file on Brock and read over it as I wait. While skimming over the details, I see he's had a few assaults on his record, but nothing as bad as this one. While it appears he was the victor, most of the others were nothing more than a standard fist fight and everything got resolved in the end. However, one case sticks out to me. There's been quite a bit removed, but I see that a full-grown man was sent to the hospital. I can also see where the judge ordered him on probation and made him go to therapy. It looks like he completed everything, but I can't find the details. I'll have to get into it when I get back to the office and see if I can dig up the rest of the file.

I make note of his address and prepare to leave when his father's file catches my eye. I open it and feel disappointed when I read what he did to young Brock.

Ted Williams was a genuine piece of shit. Not the baseball player Ted, Brock's dad. There were many reports taken of his abuse on each of the children and the mother. He's been to jail for DUI and theft, outside of the domestic calls. My heart drops from my chest when I read a report about his possible sexual assault against his own child. My stomach churns at the thought of this young man having lived through that, and my heart breaks for him. As a Christian, I try not to damn individuals, but this one is tough. He left a few years back and is currently in holding down south while he awaits trial for rape. I shake my head as I secretly pray that he spends the rest of his life behind bars. No man should ever be allowed to inflict this much damage on his fellow man, especially against their own family. My heart breaks for Brock, but I need to find him. He needs to answer for his actions.

The Williams house is a rundown shanty in the middle of town. There are beautiful houses on either side and all around, and I can't help but notice how it sticks out like it's a sore thumb. The yard is perfectly manicured and I see small repairs in an attempt to maintain the home and outbuildings, but it appears like they don't have enough money.

I climb onto the front porch and knock on the door. The front door has large open window panes, covered by a small, but dirty curtain. It's drawn open and I can see all the way to the back of the house. I spot someone sitting in a recliner. It's a woman, and she is still wearing a nightgown. She leans forward and I can see her staring back at me.

I knock again and announce myself. "Mrs. Williams. This is Chief Kelley Page. I'd like to speak with you about Brock."

She doesn't move, and I wait. She simply sits there, staring at me, and doesn't rise to answer the door. "Mrs. Williams," I repeat. "I need you to come to the door."

A shadow appears from the back of the house and approaches the woman's side. It's a male and somewhat large compared to her, but I can't make out the exact size. He stands next to the woman in the chair and appears to be in conversation. I knock again. He glances up and I see him move toward the door. He appears hesitant as he approaches.

"Hello Blake," I greet after he pulls the door open. "I'm Chief Kelley Page..."

He cuts me off. "Brock's not here."

I smile, hoping to ease the tension. "May I come in?"

He glances backward, toward the woman in the chair. "Let her in," she grumbles. "We have nothing to hide."

Blake steps to the side, and I pull open the screen door. It's an old door with a wood frame with the mesh torn around the corners. It appears to have been repaired with duct tape, at some point, but the adhesive has come undone. The spring squeaks as I pull it open and it slams shut behind me. I feel a little embarrassed, having allowed the door to hit as hard as it did, and I pray it didn't cause any damage. I don't think they can afford to repair it.

The house is cluttered and warm inside. I hear the noisy hum of fans and count three as I glance around. The smell is awkward and offensive. I pick up the distinct smell of cigarette smoke as I watch the mother pull a long drag while I look at her. I smell dust and mold. This house hasn't been cleaned thoroughly in a very long time.

"Brock ain't here."

I step closer as Blake hangs behind me and I turn, keeping eye contact with each of them. "Do you know where he is?" I ask.

"Probably with Caden," she answers. "He's always with Caden, and I think he just likes being around the wealthy. He's too good for us."

She is a chubby woman, and she's leaned forward in her dilapidated recliner and smokes her cigarette. The ash is nearly an inch long, and I feel like she needs to flick it in the ashtray before it falls to the floor. I know her name is Missy, from the file I read, and figure that her picture needs updated. This is a much older woman than the file indicates. Her nightgown is burgundy in color, and thick. Something women wore in the eighties, I think, and probably in a cooler climate. Although the lighting is dim, I notice her wrinkled skin and weathered face. She's had a hard life, and it shows. The nightgown zips down the front and her sweaty bosom almost falls out. She has a tattoo on her right breast. A bird, I think, maybe a cardinal.

"I need to locate him," I continue. "I have some questions."

"He ain't here," she repeats, once again cutting me off. "I already told you that."

I glance back at Blake. "Blake, I know you were at the diner with him."

Blake crosses the floor, going out of his way to not come close to me, before taking a seat on the sofa. "So," he expresses. "He is my brother. We eat together almost every day."

I inhale deeply, attempting to gain my patience. This family has been through a lot and I feel for them. However, I need to find Brock.

"I need you to tell me where to find him," I say. "We need to get this put behind us."

Blake shrugs his shoulders. "I don't know where he is."

I nod. "OK," I continue. "Where do you think he is?"

Blake is a larger kid, for his age, and appears uncomfortable. His face is stern, but behind it, I can see that he cares for his brother and I probably won't get anything out of him. He shrugs his shoulders again, but remains quiet.

"Do you know you can be charged with accessory?" I ask calmly. "We know you were there, and you need to help me locate your brother."

Missy remains quiet and only stares at Blake, seeming to allow him to speak for himself. He stands to his feet and walks across the room to stand in front of me. I feel uneasy as he holds his hands out in front of himself. "Arrest me then," he states coldly. "I don't know where he is, but if I did, I wouldn't tell you shit."

I smile. I can appreciate his loyalty to his brother and it makes me remember something I learned in the academy. A sibling, that's treated well will never turn on their loved ones, especially if they're poor. They have a pure hatred for the system and find solace in protecting one another.

I sigh aloud and step forward. Although I'm nervous, I stare down my nose at him and puff out my chest. "I don't want to arrest you, Blake," I admit. "I don't even want to arrest your brother. But if that young man dies, both of you will be arrested for murder." I reach into my pocket and pull out a card before offering it to him. "I just want to help."

I see the fear in his eyes as they well up with tears. "I really don't know where he is and I'm worried about him too," he mutters.

I place my arm on his shoulder. "I believe you," I reply. "But if you can get a message to him, have him call me." I exhale heavily through my nose. "It's important we get his cooperation."

Blake puts his head down. "I will."

After patting him on the shoulder, I thank each of them for their time and turn toward the door. "Check Caden's," Missy calls out. "Guarantee, he's with him."

I glance back and watch as Blake glares at his

mother. "Mom!" he exclaims before darting his eyes toward me.

"Blake," I nod my head. "I'll be seeing you." I turn to Missy. "Ma'am. Enjoy the rest of your day."

I walk forward, out the door, and step onto the porch. After I release the screen door, it again slams shut, and I can't help but feel bad, once again. It would break my heart if I damaged it. I would pay to replace it myself. I couldn't put undue burden on these folks. They have nothing left.

As I descend the steps and step onto the lawn, I hear the screen door slam shut and turn back. It's Blake, and he appears on the verge of tears.

"He's a good guy," he mumbles as he stares at the floor of the porch. "He just gets angry sometimes, and he doesn't know how to stop it."

I turn and walk back to the bottom of the steps, staring back up at him. "I believe that," I say. "I know he's had a hard life, and he's struggling with some stuff." I soften my voice. "But he has to answer for what he's done and it'll be easier if he comes in." I shake my head and shrug my shoulders. "We all have to answer for our bad choices, Blake. He's no exception and I give you my word. I'll take care of him."

Blake lifts his eyes to look at me. "I'll find him. He'll call you."

"Thank you," I reply before turning toward my cruiser. "That'll be best for all of us."

When I climb in my car, I sit for a moment in their driveway. Partly for the air conditioning, since I grew sweaty inside, but otherwise, it is to let them know that I'm watching. I feel for their family, and I know this is not what they deserve, but I have a job to do. He did an awful thing and he must answer for it. I want to get this resolved quickly, and I need to find Brock Williams.

While opening the file on Caden Astor, I pull out my phone and call the daycare. I'm worried about my baby.

"Hello Mrs. Emily," I say. "Is Ally available?

"I'm sorry, Kelley," Mrs. Emily answers. "But Ally went home. She's not feeling well today."

"Yeah," I agree. "I saw that. I'm just calling to check on Abby. How's she feeling?"

"She's much better," she replies. "She's playing with the other children and looks like she's feeling better."

I nod and feel a sense of relief. Although I figured she'd be OK, it still worries a mother when her child is ill. "Good deal," I admit. "That makes me feel better." Not wanting to hold her up, I continue. "OK then. Thank you, and I'll be there to pick her up soon."

We say our goodbyes and hang up the phone. As I glance over at the Astor file, I notice he is almost completely clean. He had a parking ticket that was thrown out, but otherwise, an impeccable record. I read his address and realize it's not far. After backing out of the driveway, I glance back toward the Williams house to see that Blake has remained on the porch. He moved to a chair, but he still watches me intently. Get in there and get your brother to call me, I mutter to myself.

The Astor house is beautiful, and it looks as though it takes up half of the block. I wonder if they always owned this much property or if they bought it from others to expand their estate. The house is a huge, two-story and a Victorian style home. Probably built in the late eighteen hundreds, but it is well maintained. Every inch has a fresh coat of paint and the cobblestone driveway horseshoes before leading behind the house to a large garage. The grass is as green as I've ever seen, and the landscaping is perfect. Even the trees appear trimmed to perfection. This is a house, I think, and appears as though it's plucked from a movie scene.

I park out front, next to the curb, when I hear my phone ding with a notification. I open the message from Carl, just as he calls out on the radio.

"Kelly?" he simply calls out.

I scroll through the photos of the crime scene as I answer. "I'm looking at them."

I soak in each photo and search my mind for something else we might need for prosecution. He did a good job and took over a hundred photos. He used a measuring stick and really showed great detail in the images.

"How many blood samples did you take?" I ask.

"Twelve," he answers.

Content with his work, I have no choice but to applaud his efforts. I can't think of anything else we might need at this time. "Good work, Carl!"

"Thanks boss," he replies and I again imagine his smile on the other end.

While approaching the door, I hear a neighbor call out from across the street. He's a young man, probably about Caden and Brock's age. I can't make out what he says, but he is approaching quickly. I turn and meet him a short way down the drive. "What is it?" I ask.

He is all smiles as he steps in front of me and I can't help but return a smile of my own. "Sorry," he speaks up. "I said that they're not home. Bob is at the hospital. He has cancer and needs some type of treatment this afternoon. There's nobody there."

I nod, thankful he approached. I glance back toward the house and see no activity that would lead me to believe he is lying. I would've knocked for a long time and wandered aimlessly. "Thank you," I reply. "But I'm looking for Caden. You don't happen to know where I can find him, do you?"

He scrunches his nose and appears hesitant. "Is this about the party tonight?"

"I'm sorry?" I ask. "What party?"

The neighbor, who I feel that I've met before but can't place him, appears confused. "You know. The party."

I shake my head. "I don't know about any party. What party?" I repeat.

He pulls his head back and still appears confused. "I'm sorry," he answers. "What are you looking for Caden for?"

"I need to speak with him about his friend, Brock," I answer honestly. "Do you know where I can find him?"

He smiles. "Ah, Brock. I'm sure they're together."

He falls silent and I wait for him to continue as he just stands there, smiling at me. "And," I continue. "Do you know where I can find them?"

"No." He shakes his head. "But they'll be at his party later, and I'm sure you can find them there."

Again, I shake my head. "What party?"

His smile fades, and he again appears confused. "Caden's end of summer bash," he replies nonchalantly.

I shrug my shoulders and stare blankly at him. "It's out at his grandpa's cabin," he continues. "Don't worry, though. They have drivers lined up in case anyone has too much to drink."

I can't believe he's telling me this. I know the kids keep their parties a secret until the last minute, so we can't break them up. We're usually only notified when there's a noise complaint and honestly, it's not that often.

"At the cabin out on Maple Road?" I ask, knowing good and well that it's not on Maple Road.

He shakes his head and grins wildly. "No," he answers. "The one on Lone Elm."

I nod and thank him for his time before turning back to my cruiser. I wonder if he told me because he wants me to break up the party, or if he's just not very bright. As soon as I get situated, I pick up my radio. "Tina, do you have a copy?"

Almost immediately, she replies. "Go ahead, chief."

I lift the radio to my mouth. "I need the address to a cabin owned by the grandpa Astor."

I pull out of the drive as she answers. "Yeah. I know right where it is. Give me a minute while I get the address." She hesitates for a moment. "Chief?"

"Yeah," I respond.

"I talked to the doctor at the hospital and it looks like Rob is going to be alright. He has a concussion, a broken nose, and a broken jaw, outside of an absolute beating, but he's awake and fine. Just hurting."

I smile upon hearing the news. As I drive through town and while I wait on the address, I key the mike again. "Carl, do you have a copy?"

"I have the address when you're ready," Tina returns.

"Go for Carl," I hear.

"Carl, go to the hospital and get the victim's statement," I respond. "Call me on my cell phone before you leave." I hesitate a moment before I hear him give me a ten-four. "OK Tina. I'm ready."

She reads me the address and I push the pedal lower, accelerating through the side streets. I smile and feel like I have him. I'm on my way to get you, Mr. Williams, I think.

The drive to the cabin is short and I almost miss my turn as GPS leads me a little further than it should have. These rural places aren't exact when it comes to GPS, but I'm able to spot the gate and find the mailbox, just beside it. The driveway is long and winding, and I finally spot the cabin in a clearing just ahead.

After pulling alongside the cabin, I pick up my radio and hold it in my hand as I step out. There are no vehicles anywhere, and there's no garage to hide them. As a matter of fact, with the woods surrounding this place, I wonder how they're going to hold all the cars for a party.

I climb the steps to the cabin and listen intently. Nothing but the sound of the water flowing behind me. I knock on the door and wait for a response. Again, there's nothing. I walk to the end of the porch and stare through the window. It's dark inside, only illuminated by the sunlight as it shines through the windows. I return to the door and twist the knob. It opens and I push it forward. The door creaks as it slowly opens to the inside. I step forward, standing inside someone else's house.

"Hello," I call out. "Police Chief Kelley Page. Is anyone home?"

I listen for a moment before walking to the middle of the room. "Hello," I repeat. "Is anyone here?"

Again, I hear nothing as I peek around. There are multiple liquor bottles lined up on the counter, with cups placed next to them. The cabin is small, with one bedroom, and one restroom outside of the large living area, with a small kitchen attached. I clear it in no time and I can determine that no one is present. I return to the porch and find multiple coolers, stocked with beer, but there isn't any ice. I step off the porch and notice the giant speakers set on pedestals. They have a tag and I recognize it as a stamp from the local high school. Great, I think. Now I'm going to have to arrest this kid for stealing speakers from the school. That'll be fun.

I glance around and listen to the silence of the place. The water flows from the creek and it mixes with the squawking of birds and buzzing of insects. Otherwise, this place is deserted and I feel that I've beaten them back. They'll be here, I think. I just need to wait.

I walk toward the creek, feeling the heat of this smoldering sun overhead. Before I reach the water's edge, I notice the clothing. First, I see a worn-out pair of dirty blue jeans, but soon recognize the bloodstains on the tee shirt as it lies to the side. I step closer and squat low to get a better look. Sure enough, that's blood and most likely, that's Brock's clothing. Feeling energized, I jog back to my cruiser and retrieve a large evidence bag and a pair of gloves.

After bagging the evidence, I walk along the edge of the creek, along the gravel bar, and find solace as the water flows. I know I have him and it's just a matter of time before he shows up. I will have Brock Williams arrested and booked into jail, all before dinnertime.

After a long wait, I feel the effects of the sheer temperature outside. I dress for professionalism and not for comfort, especially in this kind of heat. Hesitantly, I return to the cruiser and climb inside. The cold air is perfect and I soak it up. I wish this kid would come on, so I can get this over with. I toss the evidence bag of clothing to the passenger seat. As it hits, I see Brock's phone light up and hear the ding of a text message. I reach over and pick it up before bringing it to eyesight.

"Good deal. Love you."

The message is from Caden and I feel confused. Before I'm able to assess it, another message dings.

"Sorry. Mean for Ally."

Why would Caden message Brock's phone, I wonder? If he's sitting there with him, there would be no reason for him to text Brock's phone. Unless, I think. He was here, and Caden took him somewhere else. My mind wanders. Who is Ally? Surely that's not my Ally from the daycare. I feel my eyes go wide as it hits me all at once. Of course, it's her. She's the same age as the two of them, and he's probably hiding out at her house. Everyone knew he'd be with Caden, but they'd never think to look at Ally's.

My heart races as I turn around and begin down the driveway. "Tina, do you have a copy?"

I speed down the driveway and turn onto the main

road before she answers. "Go for Tina."

"I need an address for Ally Carpenter," I shout into the mic.

"Ole Ally," she replies. "She's such a good girl."

"I just need the address," I bark in return.

"Yes ma'am," she says and I hope she picked up on the seriousness in my voice. "534 Birch Street."

"Thank you," I voice before dropping the radio on the sacks of evidence next to me.

I hear her give me a 'you're welcome', but I focus on the road. I drive well above the speed limit, and my heart races in feeling that I've caught him, and I'm not that far away. I cut through the side streets and barely slow at stop signs. I would pull people over for driving as I am, but I can't help it. I need to catch Brock Williams.

As I pull up to Ally's house, I park directly behind the car that I know to be hers. It's at the daycare, every day when I drop off my child. Walking briskly, I cross the lawn and climb the stairs to the porch. Without hesitation, I ring the doorbell and begin knocking on the door. I step back a few steps. The anticipation is killing me. I again approach the door and ring the doorbell. As I knock, the door opens and an older gentleman pokes his head out. I pull open the screen door and step forward.

"I'm looking for Ally."

He stares at me wide eyed. Maybe he senses my anxiety or perhaps he knows why I'm here and Brock is in there.

I repeat myself. "I'm looking for Ally."

He points to my left. "She went for a walk in the park," he says. "She just left a few minutes ago."

I step back and glance down the street. I don't see her, but I know where the park is.

"What is this about?" he calls out behind me.

I say nothing else to him. I turn and jog down the

steps, back to my cruiser. I put it in reverse and back out of the driveway, turning the cruiser in the direction he pointed.

When I pull up to the stop sign, I catch sight of Caden's red Jeep. It's parked against the curb, directly in front of the park, so I pick up my radio.

"Carl, do you copy?"

"Go for Carl."

"Cancel that trip to the hospital," I say. "I think I found him. They're at the community park on Birch."

"Ten-four," he replies. "I'm turning around and will be there in ten minutes."

I pull up behind Caden's Jeep and lift the radio back to my mouth. "Tina," I voice. "I need a vehicle identification."

"Ready when you are," she replies.

I read her the tag number wait for the confirmation. Within moments, she sounds out on the radio that it is, in fact, registered to Bob Astor, Caden's father.

"Tina," I speak into the radio. "I'm stepping out of my cruiser at the community park on Birch. I'll have my radio with me, but I'm in pursuit."

I hear her acknowledge my statement as I climb out and look around. There's not a single person in the park. Puzzled, I glance around, hoping for some clue as to their location. I'm hot and the sun is overwhelming. I walk forward, toward the swings. I hear screaming. It's light, but I hear it.

It's coming from the woods and as I scan the tree line, I see an opening, so I take off for it. Sure enough, it's a trail and I still hear screaming. I draw my pistol and cautiously make my way up the trail. The trail is narrow, surrounded by woods and mostly uphill, but the voices are getting louder. I hear a commotion and it sounds like fighting.

My heart dances inside my chest as I near the end of the trail. I hear a gunshot. I exhale as I crest the hill and step into the open. My breathing calms as I scan with my eyes. Almost instantly, I'm drawn to a man holding a pistol and screaming loudly. I lift my gun.

"Put the weapon down!" I shout.

He turns to me. His face is weary and haggard. I don't recognize him. His beard is overgrown. His eyes spill tears down his cheeks while his lips quiver wildly and I watch them as they form his words.

"I will end this!" he yells. "I will end this abomination!"

He turns and lifts his weapon. Without another thought, I point my pistol at him and scream out before firing two shots. His body recoils and drops to the ground. I shuffle toward him and kick the gun in his hand. I point my pistol directly at his face.

He rolls over, squirming in anguish as I stand over him. He lifts his empty hands to his face and cries. I glance sideways and see the terrified eyes of the children as they embrace one another. I stop at Brock. He is horrified and kneels at the ground. Caden runs past me and I follow him with my eyes to find the slumped body of Ally lying a few feet away.

Horrified, my eyes turn toward the bound and tangled body of a human being lying at beside Ally. A duct tape wrapped hood covers the face with their arms hidden behind their back. Their legs are bent at the knees with the feet lying somewhere underneath. Their shorts are soaked, and the smell is putrid. I smell piss. I smell shit. The body is nearly folded and doesn't look like it should lie this way. Their shirt is rolled up, exposing a ghostly white belly, covered in scrapes and scratches with fresh blood oozing from the skin. They're not moving.

I'm shocked and horrified. I turn to look at the

others. The two girls still hold on to one another on the ground. Caden kneels alongside Ally and grips her in his arms. I don't comprehend. I turn to Brock. Standing to his feet, he cries like a little boy. His bottom lip quivers as he stares at me, seeming to wait for my movement. My stomach churns. I didn't expect this.

I turn back to the hooded body and see movement. I holster my pistol and roll them over. I reach for the covering over their head and lift. It's securely fastened, so I search for the end of the tape. Grabbing ahold, I unwrap, and unwrap the tape as it covers the hood. I'm amazed at how many layers were used to secure it in place. Eventually, enough is unraveled that I'm able to pull off the covering and notice that it's a simple pillow case. Something similar to what I have in my home, just like most people across this country.

I hear the loud gasp of air and heavy breathing as I lift the pillow case from their face. Staring back at me, wide eyed and horrified, is the face of the boy I met just a few hours earlier in the pharmacy. Tears pour from his eyes and, although he gasps at air, he rolls to his side and vomits immediately. I hear him sobbing loudly as he attempts to catch his breath.

"Why would you do this to me?" he cries profusely.

Brock kneels beside him and unwraps his hands as I drop to my knees to check on Ally. The boy curls in a ball, similar to a fetal position, and cries out in terror. Brock drops to his backside and sits on the ground beside him, gently rubbing his back and he, himself, cries loudly.

I kneel next to Ally and turn her over. She breathes and her eyes are open. Although she's visibly in pain, I see life. I frantically search her body and find blood near her shoulder. It's her collar bone, and the bullet went all the way through. I remove my blazer and lay it over her wound.

"Keep pressure on this," I order to Caden

His face is filled with horror, but he nods. I stand to my feet and pull my radio out before increasing the volume.

"Tina. Do you have a copy?"

"Go ahead, chief."

I take a deep breath and thunder into the radio. "I need paramedics and first responders to the community park on Birch. We're in the woods to the west side of the swing set. There's an opening at the edge and you'll find a path that leads you to me."

I hear her give me a ten-four as I look around at the faces of the six youths who are now positioned around me. I take another deep breath as I continue. "I need Carl out here, now! Call Paul and get him in early! Wake up the mayor and get me some help here! Two people have gunshot wounds, and a juvenile is severely assaulted."

I glance back at the man lying on the ground. "Get me paramedics! Get me somebody!"

I breathe in through my nose as I step forward. I roll the man to his side before pulling his hands behind his back and handcuffing him.

After I put the handcuffs on, he sobs uncontrollably.

"I was just," he calls out. "I was just going to end this abomination."

I move my eyes to the victim that I found, bound and gagged, and watch as he struggles to sit up. He is wide eyed and horrified as he looks at the suspect, handcuffed on the ground. I notice in his eyes when they recognize the assailant. He mutters something quietly and I don't know what he says. His hands and knees shake wildly and he appears on the verge of collapse. Frozen in place, I watch as he lumbers to his hands and knees and crawls across the ground. Tears stream from his face and I watch droplets fall to the ground, stirring up small speckles of dust as they land.

The assailant lifts his head as the victim makes his way in front of him before collapsing to his side. He lifts his shaky hand out and brushes it against the handcuffed assailant's cheek, wiping away the man's tears.

"I forgive you, dad," the victim whispers. "I love you."

Daryl Walker

After pulling up to the curb, I tilt the bottle to the sky and drink the last drop of the vodka. I'm here and it's time to end this. I cut the ignition and stare at the house that I once called home. I have no love here. This is a place of sin and they ruined my life. I intend to make them pay for it. I reach in the passenger seat and pick up the pistol. After transferring it to my other hand, I grab the bag and reach for the door handle.

To my surprise, I see my daughter exit the door and bound down the steps. She looks right at me and I drop my head, hoping not to be noticed. After a few moments, I glance back up. Look at her, I think. What an abomination. She is dressed like a boy and doesn't understand what she's done.

Where is she going, I wonder? Panic sets in. I want to end this and I want to do it now. I watch as she bounds down the sidewalk. I don't want to wait any longer. I should get out and end this now.

Her attention turns toward Jim Carpenter, and I see him standing on the porch, talking with her. He should be ashamed of himself. I thought he was a God-fearing man and here he is, talking with that. I should put a bullet in his head, just as payment for his blasphemy.

I watch as she continues down the sidewalk and keep my eyes focused on her. I'm going to kill her today and I will get her mother, too. I will get both of them for what they've done to me. In the end, I will take the lives of all three of us and this world will not miss us at all. I pray the Lord absolves me in the end, but I did not do my job as the man of this house. I did not keep the devil at bay.

She's getting farther away. I attempt to start the car. It won't roll over. "Come on!" I scream and pound at the steering wheel.

I try again and feel relieved when it fires up. I put it in gear and creep forward. It's so hot and the air flow calms me. I drive slowly behind, sitting at the stop sign longer than I want. Her big body lumbers to carry her faster and I hate it. I hate the sight of her.

She turns into the park and I inch forward, progressing slowly. She is walking toward the picnic table and I watch from a distance. I pull alongside the curb and turn off the ignition. After reaching to the back seat, I pull out my last bottle of vodka. I pull the top off as I watch her take a seat at the picnic table. I need to get this over with before I lose my nerve.

I take a long swallow from the bottle and feel it burn all the way down to my stomach. The burn is no worse than the thought of what they've done to me. I watch as she takes a seat on the bench. I can't believe I'm going to do this.

Since getting released from jail, I haven't been able to find steady work. Nobody wants to hire a felon, and it's even worse when you've assaulted a child. There's no explaining to people what happened. There's no way to tell them what they've done to me.

Who am I, if not a man, for trying to bring my family back to the Lord? My daughter thinks she's a man, and her mother allows it. What a blasphemous sin, and I will end it today. When I'm done with her, I will kill her mother and end myself.

I lift my hand and watch as it trembles. What a coward, I think. You never had the fortitude to end it before, and now look at you. You can't do it.

I take another pull from the bottle and look back at my child. My baby girl. Just look at her. She's a full-grown man. I shudder at the sight of her.

I can't get work. I can't get right with the Lord. What else am I to do? I will fix this and everyone will see that I'm a man of action. I can take care of my household.

She rises from the bench, and I watch her walk toward the woods. After hesitating for a moment, she passes through, and I know where she goes. She is off to her and her friend's special hideout. I know it all too well.

I step out of the car and second guess myself. What if her friends are there, I wonder? I don't care; I say to myself. They can watch her die and I will kill them too if they get in the way. A man must tend to his family!

I swallow the last of the vodka and pick up my pistol. My hand shakes violently as I reach for the bag. I take a deep breath before stepping out.

After crossing the road, I feel sick to my stomach and vomit on the sidewalk. Not wanting to lose sight, I wipe my mouth and ran to the spot that I saw her enter. It's hot and I'm winded as I reach the opening. Without another thought, I duck inside and climb the trail to the top. I'm running at almost full speed as I burst through the opening and pull back my pistol as I swing it forward, contacting the back of her head.

She slumps forward, falling hard to the ground. I drop the bag and pull out the pillowcase. After putting it in my teeth, I grab the roll of duct tape and move toward her. She's already beginning to squirm, so I kneel beside her and drop the roll of tape to the ground as I slide the pillowcase over her face. She lifts her hands, so I grab ahold and have to drop the pistol as I grip tightly and pull them behind her back. I roll her over and she speaks. I don't hear her words as I pin her hands and reach out for the tape. Quickly, I roll it around and around until her hands are secure.

I lift her head and grab at her face. She bites down on my fingers and the pain runs through me. I scream and punch her in the head. Pulling back for a moment, I shake my hand to remove the pain. Knowing that I have no time to spare, I lift her head back up and roll the tape around and around her head. I don't want to see her face when I do this. I can't look into her eyes. Her eyes are still that of my child.

I stand and feel the pain burning in my finger. I step forward and kick as ferociously as I've ever kicked. She retracts from the pain I inflict. I pick up my pistol and walk around for a moment. The pain shooting down my finger increases my anger.

"You sinful bitch!" I shout as I step forward and punch with everything I have.

Anger consumes me and I need to get this done. I will kill her and then I can get her mother. This will all be over soon.

I hear screaming and turn to see her friends. There are too many of them and I only have six bullets in this gun.

"What are you doing?" One calls out. "Stop it," another one yells.

I scream back but continue my work. Two boys attack me and I hit one with the pistol and throw the other to the side. Nothing can stop me from doing what I came here to do.

I reach down and grab hold of her. I struggle to lift her to her knees. She is heavy, and I groan as I position her upright. I lift the gun to her head and watch as she pisses herself. I feel bad for her. Sit still, I think. This will all be over soon.

My eyes fill with tears as I point the pistol at her head. The barrel shakes uncontrollably and put another hand on to steady it. I close my eyes and squeeze the trigger. "Goodbye, my girl," I whisper.

I hear her scream out as the gun fires. When I open my eyes, I see the Carpenter girl rolling to the ground as my daughter falls to her back. When she rolls to a stop, she scampers back toward the fallen body of my child. "Leave Sam alone!" she screams.

I step forward and lean down, pushing my gun near to my daughter's head. Ally clamors toward me and grabs at my leg.

"Stop it!" she shouts. "Leave my friend alone!"

I see the bullet hole in her shoulder and hate that she had to get hurt. Ally was always a good girl, and she was a good friend to my Samantha. It's nice to see that never changed.

I sob loudly as I push my pistol closer. I take a deep breath as I prepare to end her life. I close my eyes and pray.

"Put the weapon down!"

I turn to see a young woman. She is wide eyed and has her gun pointed toward me. I recognize the badge on her belt and I know it's over. This is where I end my life, and I had so much to do. What a shame, I think.

Without another thought, I turn my pistol toward her.

The "Big Five" Personality Traits

Openness:

This trait reflects an individual's willingness to try new things, enjoy new experiences, and be curious about the world around them.

Conscientiousness:

This trait describes individuals who are responsible, organized, disciplined, and hardworking.

Extroversion:

This trait characterizes individuals who are sociable, outgoing, and enjoy the company of others.

Agreeableness:

This trait reflects a person's tendency to be cooperative, friendly, and compassionate.

Neuroticism:

This trait describes individuals who are more prone to experiencing negative emotions like anxiety, worry, and sadness.